of Special Importance to our American Readers

The Case of the 24 MISSING TITLES ...

Over the years many of our American readers have been distressed that Harlequin Romances were published in Canada three months ahead of the United States release date.

We are pleased to announce that effective April 1972 Harlequin Romances will have simultaneous publication of new titles throughout North America.

To solve the problem of the 24 MISSING TITLES (No. 1553 to No. 1576) arrangements will be made with many Harlequin Romance retailers to have these missing titles available to you before the end of 1972.

Watch for your retailer's special display!

If, however, you have difficulty obtaining any of the missing titles, please write us.

Yours truly,

The Publisher
HARLEQUIN ROMANCES.

OTHER
Harlequin Romances
by MARJORIE NORRELL

Many of these titles are available at your local bookseller,
or through the Harlequin Reader Service.

For a free catalogue listing all available Harlequin Romances,
send your name and address to:

HARLEQUIN READER SERVICE,
M.P.O. Box 707, Niagara Falls, N.Y. 14302
Canadian address: Stratford, Ontario, Canada.

or use order coupon at back of book.

DR. MAITLAND'S SECRETARY

by

MARJORIE NORRELL

HARLEQUIN BOOKS   TORONTO
WINNIPEG

Original hard cover edition published in 1971
under the title "The Doctor's Secretary"
by Mills & Boon Limited, 17-19 Foley Street,
London   W1A 1DR, England

© Mills & Boon 1971

Harlequin edition published April, 1972

SBN 373-01577-1

*All the characters in this book have no existence outside the
imagination of the Author, and have no relation whatsoever to
anyone bearing the same name or names. They are not even
distantly inspired by any individual known or unknown to the
Author, and all the incidents are pure invention.*

Printed in Canada

CHAPTER ONE

"I TOLD you it would be more fun here at home than in some stuffy seaside boarding house, didn't I, Molly?"

Ann Flecker turned the glance of her dancing, hazel-coloured eyes on her friend who was following surely, if more sedately, down the long winding lane from the farmhouse.

"It's very good of your people to have me here for a holiday like this." Molly Watson spoke, as always, quietly, but her oval-shaped face framed in the long dark-gold hair, loosened now from its customary nurse's cap, was strangely contented. "If only Flint could have had his vacation at the same time . . ." she was continuing, but Ann cut her short, her gay laughter ringing through the distant sounds of activity from the farm-yard.

"Flint by name and Flint by nature. That's what they say about him at Tunby General, you know!" she teased. Then her glance softened as she saw the hurt look in her friend's eyes.

"I was teasing," she said quickly, trying to cover up the momentary embarrassment. "It always amazes me what you two see in one another! He's only got one idea in his head—apart from those about *you*, of course—and that's to get to the top of the tree as a surgeon! He'll do it, of course, but I would never have expected him to give up the opportunity of being with Sir Alistair Grahame for a full month, not if he'd been offered the Crown Jewels!"

"I know." Molly sighed. "It was too good an opportunity to miss and I'd have been selfish if I'd objected. . . ."

"You, selfish?" Ann's tone told more plainly than words could ever have done just what she thought of that idea. "You wouldn't know how to begin!" she said scornfully but tenderly. "That's Flint Cardew's line, not yours! *And* he'll end with a knighthood or something like that of his own before he's finished, I'd like to bet! How'll you like being Her Ladyship or whatever you'll be then?"

"It might never come to that," Molly sighed, "but it would be wonderful—for Flint—if it does. He'd like it more than anything, I think," she added with customary honesty. "I'm not in the least certain it would be anything in my line, though! I'd be scared stiff. I'd much rather have a life like your mum's," she went on, dreamily, Ann noted. "She must have enjoyed every moment. She was telling me this morning how she'd worked as district nurse around here for years and years, and only gave up when you were born, after all the others had grown up! Now they'd be lost without her on the farm, and everyone seems to come to her, not just when they're in trouble, either."

"Oh," Ann dismissed the sincere praise lightly enough, but it was plain she really liked to know her mother's unfailing courage and cheerfulness—as well as her nursing qualities—were appreciated, "Mum's Mum to the entire village, I should think. She's brought most of the younger ones into the world, and helped to see a lot of the older ones' parents and so on out of it. They all know her, they all think of her as a friend, and when Dad died," her voice choked a moment and then she continued steadily, "and Tim had to take over Beckside

6

Farm, everyone came round to see if they co⌐
and a lot of them did. It was partly because Mu⌐
how fond Tim is of horses and how he hopes to f⌐
own stock here and breed that she's encourag⌐
latest idea of his, though I'm not so sure it'll all w⌐
as Tim hoped."

"Why shouldn't it work out?" Molly asked curi⌐
as she followed Ann through the farm gate the othe⌐
carefully fastened behind them.

"I don't think Mum's very keen on this new stall⌐
he's bought, somehow," Ann confided, adding in a li⌐
confidential rush, "Mum's a queer person, you kno⌐
I'm sure if she'd lived in the Middle Ages she'd ha⌐
been burned as a witch! She gets...what do you call
'em?...premonitions or something, and she's got a real
one about this horse. Says it'll bring no luck and that she
can see accidents and heartache and I don't know what
ahead unless Tim gets rid of it, and that's about the last
thing he wants to do. Personally I think the horse's name
has something to do with her 'premonition'," she concluded.

"What is its name?"

"Satan," Ann said decisively. "And he's coal black,
with a wickedly rolling eye. I don't like the look of him
much myself. I shall be content if Tim lets me go on
riding old Bess. He can keep that mettlesome brute to
himself, so far as I'm concerned. I like a nice, steady
jog-trot. Not a mad dash! Tim swears he'll master
Satan, but according to Mum it's more than likely Satan
will end up being master of Tim!"

"Not necessarily," Molly said slowly. "I remember
when I was much younger, and Dad was in Canada for
some time, there was a horse like that where we were
stationed, and all he wanted was someone with a firm

hand, and who wasn't frightened of him. That's most important," she said decisively. "Perhaps Satan knows he's got most of you scared of him, and he enjoys it. Where is he? I'd like to see him."

"You'll see him, all right," Ann affirmed. "You said you'd like to ride, and Tim's given me no peace until I promised to bring you down to the stables one morning. If I were you I'd stick to Prince," she cautioned. "Anyhow, Tim'd never let you try to ride Satan. He's determined to master him himself."

"Perhaps he doesn't require 'mastering'," Molly reiterated. "Just understanding. Anyhow, I'm longing to see him."

Ann made no further comment about the horses but chatted of the farm and the people who worked on it and lived in its bounds, explaining as they went along down to the paddock that since her great-grandfather had first farmed here the place had been handed down, generation after generation, each new owner adding something different, some stamp of his own.

"Tim's determined to make the breeding of bloodstock his memorial, as it were," she said as she opened the gate that led into the paddock and to the stables. "He'll do it too. He's horse-crazy!"

They spent a happy half hour or so wandering from stall to stall and one velvety nose after another protruded in search of the sugar lumps and apples which Ann always brought with her. There was no sign of Tim, and Eric, one of the boys who worked in the stables, volunteered the information that "Master's off to see about a roan Mr. Steadman's got for sale. Said he won't be back till late," he told them.

Ann nodded gravely, but Molly wasn't even listening. She was talking to a proud-looking horse whose eyes

glinted as she spoke, and who eyed her speculatively as she advanced, not yet venturing to stroke his nose.

"That's Satan!" Ann said in a scared whisper. "Come away, Molly! Nobody goes near him now, except for Tim."

"Then it's high time someone else learned to make friends with him, poor darling!" Molly said quietly, advancing confidently, still talking quietly to the huge horse.

Satan's ears pricked and his eyes rolled, but he didn't make a sound. After a short interval, talking quietly all the time, Molly put out a cautious hand and gently stroked his nose. The huge creature seemed to relax and to really enjoy the attention he was receiving, and after a moment or two Ann too seemed to breathe more easily although she still kept her distance.

"Come away, love!" she urged in her soft, Yorkshire tones. "I know we can't really trust him!"

"I do!" Molly said suddenly. She turned to the stable man and the two boys who were watching as though they could not credit what they were actually seeing.

"Won't one of you saddle him for me, please?" she asked. "Or shall I do it myself?"

For a moment no one spoke, then Ann broke into protests which, to Molly's trained ear, revealed more than a hint of hysteria. As the younger of the two boys came hesitantly forward Ann clutched his arm.

"Mr. Tim'll be angry...." she was beginning, but without appearing rude the boy carefully lifted her detaining fingers from his arm and said quietly:

"I don't think so, Miss Ann. Mr. Tim was saying this morning it was time someone else could ride Satan because he hadn't the time to give him the exercise he needs, not these days, with all the harvest just ripening

9

and so on. I've been trotting him round the yard, but that isn't enough. If the young lady's used to horses. . . ."

"I used to ride at home," Molly said quickly, "before Dad was posted abroad again, and I've ridden when he was in Canada. I've not always had a jog-trot mount, either, and I'm certain Satan and I are going to be good friends."

As though he could understand what was being said the horse stood quite still as he was saddled, although he looked from one to the other of the girls as though assessing what they might be thinking. Ann stood a little apart, not quite wringing her hands but with anxiety and unease in every line of her slight frame. When Satan was ready Sam, the boy who had saddled him, helped Molly mount, and with a toss of his head Satan trotted out through the gates of the yard exactly as though he knew where he intended to go.

Molly felt suddenly free, free as, she realised abruptly, she had not felt since the day Flint Cardew had slipped the engagement ring on to the third finger of her left hand.

It was a strange and deliciously exciting sensation, and it seemed that something of her new-found joy communicated itself to her mount. Satan seemed to sense her sudden joy, and to be enjoying himself equally, for he tossed his head and went off down the lane, his easy trot changing and quickening as he felt Molly's own confidence as though there were some secret communication between rider and horse.

In one of the fields further down the lane a party of picnickers had descended from their car and were encamped on the grassy verge, looking like well-to-do gipsies. Molly noted the small party with the same sense of amused tolerance which she had surveyed Satan.

There was a lady who was obviously 'Mother', keeping a watchful eye on the spirit stove. Father and two teenage children were playing some ball game, but there did not appear to be any menace there. Three younger ones, a small, lonely-looking boy and a pair of girls equally obviously identical twins, were 'helping' unpack the food hamper.

As Satan and Molly approached the small boy looked up with interest. Without warning he stooped and picked up a fairly large paper bag which had apparently contained part of the picnic fare, and, his small round cheeks bulging with the effort, he blew the bag up until it was distended to its fullest size.

Molly did not even think of any possible effect on Satan. The next moment there was a loud report as the child burst the bag between clenched hands, then Satan was careering down the narrow road as though possessed.

Molly exerted all her strength, but to no avail. She had been so startled by Satan's sudden bolting that she had lost both stirrups and clung desperately to the pommel of the saddle. She was both angry and a little frightened. It was one thing to have been riding Satan while he was under her complete control and quite another to be astride this creature which seemed completely possessed.

The road terminated in a narrow lane down which they charged at a fast gallop. There was a gate at the end of the lane, but apparently this presented no difficulty to the stallion. The mad charge continued down the narrow lane, until suddenly the trees on either side seemed to close in on Molly, and her face was whipped by low-hanging branches.

It was much later, after what Tim jokingly called 'the inquest', that they discovered the laceration in Satan's side, a laceration caused by a loose piece of fencing. That must have been the final straw to what the horse felt to have been a nightmarish morning. With a strange falsetto squeal he shied violently, just as Molly was caught on the shoulder by a low branch of a tree. She felt a violent pain in her neck and shoulder, and the next second she was thrown fiercely to the ground, where she lay moaning as Satan, unheeding, galloped onwards, she knew not where.

She seemed to have lain there for hours. Afterwards she was told that Satan galloped back to the farm by another route, one which he must have taken automatically, and that once he arrived there, riderless, Tim, now returned, and some of the men went out in immediate search for Molly.

Ann was with them when she was found. Apart from her shoulder and the pain in her neck she felt curiously numb from the waist downwards, and even though she was frightened and in pain, the nursing side of her inner self knew instinctively that something was seriously the matter.

"My back. . . ." she said feebly to Ann, as the other girl stooped, white-faced, above her. "It doesn't feel right. . . ."

"We'll take you home, love," Ann began soothingly, but Tim, white-faced even under his tan, cut her short.

"We'll take her to the Cottage," he said briefly but with authority. "Dr. Maitland had better look at her as soon as possible."

"I want Flint," Molly said stubbornly, and, ignoring her brother's frown, Ann swiftly assured her that he would be sent for at once. Molly found herself carefully lifted on to an improvised stretcher, then Tim drove the station waggon carefully out of the lane, down the narrow country road and finally to the main road which led to the village of Bronton where the Cottage Hospital was situated.

Afterwards Molly told Ann she had not remembered much of the journey or of her arrival at the Cottage. She had been only partially conscious during the journey, and when she was lifted from the station waggon she had lost consciousness altogether, which, as Ann remarked cheerfully, was in reality a blessing.

When she was finally able to realise her surroundings, she discovered she was in the universally adopted high, narrow hospital bed, and that a pleasant young first-year nurse was sitting beside her.

"What happened?" Molly asked, and was amazed to discover how weak her own voice sounded.

"You were thrown," the girl told her. "Don't worry too much," she advised, and neither of them saw anything in the least incongruous in her offering such consolation to one whose nursing experience so greatly exceeded her own. She offered a drink of bitter lemon and glucose, and Molly was surprised to discover how difficult it really was to drink from a feeding cup even though the liquid seemed at this point literally life-restoring.

"My back . . . ?" she began tentatively. "It . . . doesn't hurt, but I don't seem to feel. . . ."

She stopped. Somehow it made it easier not to have to say the words, to actually voice the fear which had been haunting her ever since she had felt the hard jar to her nervous system when she had hit the ground. The girl seemed to understand, and automatically Molly found herself thinking she obviously had the right instincts for her profession.

"Dr. Maitland doesn't think there'll be permanent damage," she said, then her hand flew to her lips as she

seemed to recollect that it was not her place to either
diagnose or to comment on the condition of a patient at
this stage. "I . . . it seems you'll be all right, very soon,"
she concluded in a little rush, the warm colour rising in
her cheeks so that she looked even younger than she
obviously was.

Despite her discomfort, Molly felt a stab of sympathy.
She could remember quite well what it had felt like, that
first year on the wards.

"What's your name, Nurse?" she asked quietly.

"I'm Cynthia Greenwood," the girl said, her blushes
subsiding as she realised Molly was sympathetic. "It
must be awful for you," she confided in another little
rush of words. "Being . . . sort of on the receiving end, I
mean."

"It's a change!" Molly managed wryly, smothering a
grimace of pain. Instantly the other was attentive.

"Dr. Maitland wrote up a sedative for you," she
picked up the chit. "It was after they'd X-rayed you, but
he said you'd be feeling rough when you regained consciousness and you'll need a good sleep."

Molly had the rather dreadful if vague feeling that
she would never sleep again until she knew just what
had happened and whether Flint was coming. It would
be more than awful to be asleep if he came all the way
from Edinburgh, where he had gone for a month to be
with the famous Sir Alistair Grahame!

Cynthia, she decided vaguely, and for the second time,
had certainly chosen her profession well—or it had
chosen her—for in next to no time Molly found herself
taking the two capsules of the prescribed amytal, and
before very long she was sleeping soundly. She didn't
dream, and remembered nothing more until someone
wakened her the following morning and announced that

she was Night Staff Maxwell, "Just going off duty... wanted to be certain you were all right, Nurse."

Molly returned meekly that she had slept like the proverbial log, but that she was terribly stiff.

"I should imagine you will be," Staff said comfortingly, a tone Molly recognised as one she herself had often used to patients in the past and one she would never use again, she vowed, suddenly understanding better than she had ever understood previously how impersonal that particular tone sounded in a patient's ears.

"But one can't get emotionally involved!" she reminded herself, and instantly found she was asking Staff if there had been any word from her fiancé, Mr. Cardew. "He's house surgeon at Tunby General," she explained. "We both work there, but he's away for a month on special leave."

"I haven't heard anything," Penny Maxwell said reassuringly, "but that doesn't mean a thing here. He's probably got directly in touch with Dr. Maitland. You can ask him when he comes round this morning."

There didn't appear to be any alternative to this suggestion, so Molly contented herself by thinking over all the plans she had privately made for the marvellous day when Flint obtained that for which he made no secret of the fact he was working—a place in Harley Street.

"I'm not going to end up just one amongst so many ordinary doctors and surgeons, Molly," he had said more than once. "I know I've got it in me to do something big, and I intend to do it."

Privately Molly considered her own father, a physician and surgeon with the World Health Organisation, was already doing 'something big' in the matter of healing the ills of humanity, no matter who they were or in what part of the world to which he might be sent, but she had said nothing of this to Flint. His dreams of 'something big' weren't along the same lines, and, she had made generous allowance for that fact, there had to be this kind of person in all walks of life!

Before Flint had confided a little of his personal dream to her Molly had thought of them doing something along the same lines as her own parents, for her mother was a qualified Sister and the two of them had worked all over the world for years. Evidently that sort of thing wasn't what Flint had in mind, so she had said nothing, merely waiting until events had shown whether or not the opportunities he hoped for were going to materialise.

It appeared they were well on their way to him, when he had received the invitation from the gifted Scots surgeon, to spend a month of what should have been his annual vacation, in his special clinic in Edinburgh. Molly, although she had long cherished plans of a shared holiday in the Scillies, had said nothing of her disappointment, but instead had cheerfully accepted Ann's hearty and oft-repeated invitation to spend her holidays in Bronton district, not too far from the sea and yet in the midst of what had proved to be a very pleasant countryside.

"It's as well I didn't go to Tresco," she told herself. "It might not have been easy for Flint to come there quickly. As it is, he'll be able to get a fast train nearly all the way and then a local one ... shouldn't take him long, even if he doesn't feel like the long drive!"

She lay still, accepted her breakfast when it was brought to her and wished desperately that she didn't feel so stiff, but underlying the discomfort was the thought that it couldn't be long now before Flint was there beside her bed, filling the small ward with his huge presence. She had often teased him about his size, for he was tall and broad as well, and his erect carriage made him seem even larger than he was. Now she felt she could not wait until his familiar form came through the door.

There might not be the same number of patients in the Bronton Cottage Hospital as were housed in Tunby General, but the routine and the traditionally accepted behaviour were all to the usual pattern.

Matron Roseby proved to be a middle-aged woman with a warm, kindly smile and with an apparently genuine interest in her patients when she made her round just after the day staff had settled down for the work of the day. At ten o'clock, punctual to the second, the doors opened again and the man Molly knew instinctively to be Dr. John Maitland, Tim's doctor and friend, walked in, accompanied by the Sister and the day staff nurse on duty.

He spent some time with each patient in turn, and Molly lay quite still, watching his every move, every line of emotion on his thin, clever face. She could feel the tension mounting inside herself as he drew nearer to her own bedside, but although she felt she had succeeded in controlling it completely he had spotted it at once.

"Relax, Nurse Watson!" he said kindly as he took her pulse rate. "It's a very unfortunate thing to have happened on your holiday, but it isn't the end of the world, you know! You're not irreparably damaged, if that's what's worrying you!"

"It was," Molly confessed briefly. "My back. . . ."

"Is very badly strained," he cut in briskly. "Nothing we can't cope with here. Some rest first, then some physiotherapy. . . ."

"I have to be back...." Molly was beginning anxiously, but he interrupted a second time.

"I know," he said gently, "but don't worry about that. Your Matron has given you extended sick-leave to follow your vacation, so you won't lose too much pay. In the meantime, if you'll accept what help we can give you, you should be able to do some admin. work, here, if not in Tunby, until you're well enough to go on the wards again."

"Thanks, but I'd rather not." Molly hated to sound ungrateful, especially as he was such a pleasant young man. "Once I got stuck in admin. I'd be lucky to ever get out!" she opined. "I've seen it happen to other people who've gone in on a temporary basis and remained for life, or what was left of it, if you think an inactive, sedentary job can be called living!"

"Well," he began to move away, smiling gently, "you certainly won't be feeling very much like being active for some months, Nurse," he commented. "Think it over, first, and be thankful you didn't break any bones ... or that Satan didn't trample you!"

"I ... I *am* thankful." Molly felt miserable, for she *had* sounded ungrateful, and that was the last thought in her head. "It's just ... if I could see my fiancé," she began, "or have some message from him ... *please*! They know up at the farm where he is."

"I think he has already been contacted, Nurse Watson," Dr. Maitland said formally. "I shall be round at Beckside later on this morning. I'll look in and ask if there's any message for you. I shall be back here before visiting time, so if there is I'll let you know before Mrs. Flecker and Ann come to see you, shall I?" and with that she had to be content for the time being.

* * *

By the time the general routine of the morning was over, beds tidied once again, elevenses brought round and the boy with the local newspaper delivery had been, Molly began to feel she would never forget the pattern on the ceiling of Ward Two, Bronton Cottage Hospital.

It wasn't that everyone wasn't kindness itself. They all seemed to fall over themselves to be especially pleasant, and she was ashamed of the unbidden feeling which had somehow slipped into her mind that there was some kind of conspiracy afoot to keep something—something vitally important—from her.

There was a certain amount of vague but definite emotional relief when she saw it was the young first-year nurse, Cynthia, who was bringing her lunch tray.

"Don't try to move, Nurse," the girl began, moving pillows and setling her more comfortably in quite an experienced manner. Molly's already considerable respect for the Cottage went up by leaps and bounds, and she found to her surprise that she was hungry enough to eat some of the light soup and the beautifully cooked lamb with which she was being fed.

The lamb was accompanied by small new potatoes and freshly gathered garden peas. Molly didn't need to be told they had been freshly gathered, she could distinctly remember that special flavour from her childhood days when she had spent many of her school holidays with her grandparents in the country. There was fresh mint too, and afterwards a delicious concoction of apple and creamy custard, altogether a very satisfactory meal, but one throughout which, try as she might to lead round to the subject, she found it impossible to put any direct question to Cynthia as to whether or not she imagined a conspiracy afoot.

"What time is visiting hour?" she asked as Cynthia

prepared to depart and a ward maid arrived with a steaming cup of tea.

"Two-thirty to three-thirty," Cynthia said briskly. "I expect they'll be down from Beckside. Ann will, anyway. She said so this morning when she telephoned."

"Ann ... phoned?" Molly was instantly alert. Perhaps this was the 'something' she had sensed. Maybe Satan was injured. Perhaps he hadn't just galloped back to the farm, but something had happened to him, and at the time of finding her injured no one had told her for fear of upsetting her further?

"What was wrong?" she asked anxiously. "They know where I am, and I'm certain Ann would realise it isn't anything really serious."

"She stayed until the X-rays were through, I believe," Cynthia admitted. "She knows, perhaps, more than I can tell you about what's happened to you."

"Then it isn't ... that," Molly said decisively, her glance not leaving the other girl's face for an instant. "Yet there *is* something wrong, isn't there?" she demanded. "I can't even put a mental finger on what it might be, but I *know* there's ... something not quite right! What is it? You know, don't you?" She tried to catch Cynthia's arm, but the effort made her back ache more and her shoulder throbbed so violently she felt she would faint with the sudden onset of extra pain.

"You might as well tell me," she muttered, sinking back against the pillows. "A nurse isn't like an ordinary patient ... she can be told things anyone else would worry about. ..."

"Sister O'Dare says we're to keep you quiet until Dr. Maitland's been back," Cynthia said incautiously. "He'll be here very soon. I heard him saying he'd be here before visiting time, and that's not so very far away right now."

Molly knew she couldn't argue with the girl. Cynthia, being the type of girl she was, would try to help and probably get herself into trouble with Sister. Molly knew enough about some Sisters to appreciate that all of them were not like kindly Sister Wilkes, Sister on her own ward at Tunby General.

"I'll be good," she said, half smiling, although she had never felt less like smiling in the whole of her life. "Can you persuade Sister to let me have something for this pain, though, please? When I tried to get a hold of your arm a few minutes ago I merely made matters worse! I ought to have known better."

"Dr. Maitland wrote something up for you, I know," Cynthia said. "I'll see Staff and get it for you, but *please* lie quiet, Nurse, or I'll be the one to be in trouble!"

"O.K.," Molly promised, and did her sincere best to relax, accepting the pain-killing tablet proffered by the girl. "I'll remember!"

She felt the easement of pain in a short time, and lay quietly, silently praying that Dr. Maitland would not be long delayed, or even forget he had promised to come back after he had been to Beckside Farm.

She need not have worried quite so much. When, some time later, she came to know him better, she discovered that John Maitland was the most reliable person she had ever known or *could* ever come to know, however long her life might be.

She watched his grave progress up the ward, some instinct telling her that something was wrong, that he was displeased in some way, and almost at once found herself hoping it had been nothing she had done or said which had occasioned the gravity of his expression. It was gone as he pulled up a chair to sit beside her bed. He was smiling, and his grey-blue eyes were sharing the smile from his generous mouth.

"How do you feel now, Nurse?" he asked, taking her pulse almost automatically, it seemed, since he had not even looked at her chart.

"A little better—I think," Molly said cautiously. "My shoulder hurts when I move, though."

"Not surprising," he smiled again. "You have a traumatic dislocation, and severe jarring of the vertebrae of your spine. I'm afraid you'll have to rest for some time, and then we shall have to hand you over to the physiotherapy people for further treatment before you'll be able to go back to your normal life! Don't worry," he went on kindly and quickly as he saw the change in her expression, "It might have been so much worse, you know! You could have been paralysed, or even... dead."

"I know." Molly bit her lip. She hadn't wanted to have to question him about Flint, but she *had* to know! "I'll be all right," she said firmly, "I know that, but I shall be glad when Dr. Cardew arrives. They did let him know, from Beckside, didn't they?" she added anxiously. "Ann promised...."

"Yes," John Maitland was suddenly more grave again. "Ann *did* let him know...."

"And?" Molly prompted, as he hesitated.

"You must realise, my dear," he began gently, carefully—too carefully, Molly thought—"he has been most fortunate in being able to spend this month with Sir Alistair Grahame! He can't possibly drop everything at a moment's notice."

"You mean... he isn't coming, don't you?" Molly could not keep the disappointment from her voice, and she knew her eyes had filled with tears which, despising

such behaviour, she hastily blinked away. "He isn't...
bound to Sir Alistair!"

She was well aware, after listening to so many lectures
in psychology, that she was venting her anger on the
unsuspecting bearer of the news, simply in order to hide
her real emotion of sudden despair and a truly frighten-
ing emotion which, part of her mind registered, felt she
had been badly let down. Dr. Maitland looked extremely
uncomfortable, and stirred uneasily on his chair, his face
brightening a little as a bell clanged through the
hospital, announcing time for visiting hour.

"That isn't really the point, Nurse," he rose as he
spoke, and as the doors of the ward opened to admit the
first stream of waiting visitors. "It appears they're working on some new technique or other, and naturally Dr.
Cardew is anxious to learn all he can. I'm sorry." He
looked extremely uncomfortable and distressed, as
though whatever had gone wrong might be his fault, and
Molly's warm impulsive heart felt sorry to have been the
unwitting cause of this unease.

"It ... doesn't matter," she managed a small smile
which, had she but known it, made him feel more upset
than ever, it was so patently brave. "I expect if I'd been
seriously hurt he would have come anyway. As it is ...
well, I didn't know I was going to be so fortunate, did
I? I wouldn't have made such a fuss about contacting
him, if I'd realised. It's just that ... I've no one else of
my own in England just now, and it seemed ... rather
important at the time."

"I couldn't agree more, Nurse," Dr. Maitland was
surprised by the vehemence in his own voice as he
listened to it, and as he watched her face, bravely hiding
the disappointment he knew she had felt so keenly.

"You may not have anyone of your own in England

23

right now, Nurse," he said with a smile, "but it looks as though you have friends right here in Bronton! They're coming to see you now, I believe."

Molly looked where the stream of visitors was gradually fanning out to the different bedsides along the ward. Coming towards her, their faces beaming with loving smiles, were Ann and her mother, each well laden.

"Hello, love!" Joan Flecker's comfortable figure sank down thankfully on the small hospital chair her daughter brought forward for her before crossing the ward to bring another one for herself. "That was an awful thing to happen on your holiday, wasn't it? I don't think I'm flattering anyone when I say I think, up to then, you were really enjoying yourself, weren't you?"

"Very much so, thank you, Mrs. Flecker," Molly said sincerely, "and please don't blame anyone—or Satan—it was my own fault. Ann and everyone else said I ought not to attempt to ride him, so, in a sort of way, it really serves me right! I'm only too sorry for all the trouble I've caused everyone, but at least," she said thankfully, "it seems Satan wasn't hurt at all. I'm glad about that."

"Billy Fox said there were some people having a picnic on the roadside and that a little boy burst a big paper bag with a loud bang. That was what startled Satan, it seems. It was fortunate Billy was on one of his nature-observation expeditions, or we might have been looking for you a long time before we finally found you. Billy saw you thrown, and, very sensibly, came to Beckside. He got there just after Satan had galloped home, riderless. We were worried stiff."

"I'm sorry," Molly said, inadequately she felt, but Mrs. Flecker appeared to understand. She patted the girl's hand in a comforting manner.

"Not your fault, love," she said cheerfully, "and it

might have been a good deal worse! I've always had the feeling that no good would come of having Satan in the stables, and this seems to have proved my point! Never mind, we'll soon have you home, and John can arrange for the Mobile Therapy Unit to call round at Beckside just as long as he says you'll need it. Personally, with a course of faradism, plenty of rest and proper physiotherapy—and I can assure you that that will be well taken care of—you'll be as right as rain before the end of the year."

"But it's only late August!" Molly said, aghast. "I . . . that is, we'd hoped. . . ."

She broke off. What now of the dreams she thought she had shared with Flint? His term at Tunby General ended in late September, and she had hoped he would include her in whatever plans he had made for the months which would follow. She didn't mind helping him, in any way she could, along the road of his chosen career, but now this accident had happened and he had not even been to see her . . . for all she knew, had not even telephoned. . . .

"Your fiancé," Joan, it seemed, could almost see what she was thinking, and the ready colour flew into Molly's face, only to fade almost at once, leaving her looking more white and strained than before. "Ann phoned him." Joan might appear to be speaking with a casual simplicity, but Molly knew her well enough by this time to realise she was more disturbed than anyone would have guessed by her still smiling face. "He said he was . . . very involved." She said the last two words with such significance that Molly instinctively knew there was more behind them than was plain at first. "He asked to be kept informed of your progress," Joan went on, and in anyone else Molly would have said the tone was

25

cynical in the extreme, but somehow cynicism and Joan seemed worlds apart.

"I told him we could put him up, if he wanted to come and see you, and he said he'd think about that when you come back to Beckside. I shall phone him again tonight, or Ann will, now that we've seen you."

"I can't come back to the farm like this!" Molly gesticulated in horror to her still form as it lay beneath the white covers. "Your hands are full enough as it is, with all the work on the farm and all you do for people in and around the village! I . . . there's a nurses' convalescent home I can go to. . . ."

"If you'd rather," Joan said, undisturbed, "but you did come to us for your holiday, remember! And that's not over yet! Don't worry about the work for me. Ann's home another two weeks, and she'll do any running about after you that's needed, and love it. She'll be most upset if you go away from us just because this has happened, and Tim'd say I ought not to have allowed you to go near Satan. . . ."

"I'd love to stay," Molly was anxious to stem the tide of words. Like most of her kind Joan could talk on and on, and never appeared to tire of whatever subject engrossed her at the moment. "It's just . . . you scarcely know me, and here I've landed all this extra work on to your shoulders. . . ."

"And a load of sunshine as well," Joan rose as the bell went to signal the end of the visitors' hour. "We love having you. And we feel we know you well, Ann's written so much about you since you met, and we all wanted to meet you, but not, of course, like this! Anyhow, we want you to stay long enough to know there are other delights in and around Bronton apart from trying to break your neck!"

They joined in her laughter, and as Ann stooped to say, " 'Bye for the present, love," she whispered comfortingly :

"The girl on the switchboard here is a friend of mine. I'll ring her with a message for you when I've spoken to Dr. Cardew again. All right?"

Molly nodded, but she did not want to say 'unless it's a personal message'. Ann, she felt, would understand the need for discretion, and it was comforting to know someone would keep Flint and herself in touch, even, as it were, by remote control!

"Thanks," she said quietly. "That's kind."

"I think so too," Ann said cheekily, "considering I don't think he's one half good enough for you—as a person!" and laughing at Molly's protests she followed her mother from the ward.

The evening and the week following seemed to Molly the longest time she had ever known. Her shoulder wasn't quite so painful, but her back was still troublesome, and when she first walked—with the aid of Cynthia and another first-year nurse—down the ward, she felt as though her legs didn't even belong to her.

The messages, relayed faithfully each day by Ann, were not very encouraging, even though she knew Flint, in his position, had to be extra careful both in words and actions. It wasn't much of a comfort either to be informed that he would not be coming to see her until she was out of the Cottage and once more installed at Beckside Farm.

"He says you'll understand it's difficult to get away at the moment," Ann reported when she brought this information. "I must say it's what I expected of him, but that doesn't prevent me being disappointed to find how right I am!"

27

"I can't start out by interfering in his career!" Molly protested, but all the same she felt reasonably certain in her own mind that had it been Flint who was hurt, no matter how slightly, she would have gone to him, even if she had been staying as a private guest of Matron's!

"Good thing everyone's not alike," she told herself firmly. "I know this chance means a great deal to him."

She accepted the treatment at the Cottage with her customary courage, and even though her back and shoulder seemed to ache unbearably after the first two or three treatments, she persisted and was rewarded when, at last, the muscles which had been jarred, the vertebrae which had been dashed so violently together definitely began to respond to treatment and some easement was clearly felt.

"You'll have to take things easily for at least six months, I'm afraid, Nurse," Dr. Maitland told her as he visited her for the last time in hospital. "We'll have the ambulance take you to Beckside in the morning. The Unit will be along three times the first three or four weeks, after that their treatment will tail off, as it were, until you no longer require their help. After that," he smiled, "we'll see. Certainly you won't be walking any wards for some time!"

"I don't know anything else!" Molly began to grumble, and then, half smiling, added : "I do, though. I can type, after a fashion, and I did get my first examination in speed-writing, so maybe there's something useful I can do for Ann's mum or for the farm, accounts or something, though my maths side isn't really my strong point!"

"We'll talk about that later." John Maitland looked down at her and she could have sworn there was unmistakable pity in his glance. She said, more sharply than she had intended :

"What else is it, Doctor? What haven't you told me? I'm ... going to be all right again, aren't I?" she demanded.

"Perfectly all right," he said gravely, "perhaps better than you were before all this happened. You really did need that rest, you know! You nurses are all alike, it seems. Nothing's too much trouble, and none of you spare yourselves."

"We have such a splendid example set us by the medical profession we can't let them down!" Molly said mischievously. "Thanks, though. One likes to know someone understands how the work, much as one loves it, can sometimes become a bit much, as it were."

"The rest will do you good," he reaffirmed, and went away before she remembered she had been trying to find out about that look of pity, whether it was real or imagined!

She had decided it was imagined by the time the ambulance came to take her to Beckside. The farm was waiting to welcome her, almost, she felt, as though she were another daughter of the house. Joan had baked, and a delicious scent of newly made bread and cakes hung on the air. A bed had been brought down into what Ann told her used to be known as 'the office', but Tim was not much use where paper-work was concerned, and most of it was put into his late father's roll-top desk to await the coming to Beckside of the young woman who had built up a thriving business for herself, going round most of the local farms and keeping their necessary paper-work up to date.

"She doesn't come for nearly a month, Molly," Ann told her, "so you'll be able to get upstairs by then, I expect. In the meantime, you'll be in the centre of the family life down here, much more interesting than being stuck on your own upstairs when I'm not around to come and sit with you."

The family were more than considerate. When Dr. Maitland, or the Mobile Therapy Unit arrived, everyone vanished until Joan, when she had judged almost to the second it would be safe to come in, entered with freshly brewed tea and home-made biscuits.

They were even, Molly thought, more than normally considerate when, at long last, Flint phoned to say he'd be with her late that afternoon.

All day she counted the minutes, and when Joan brought in a tea-tray she could scarcely touch a bite.

"Don't get so excited, lovey," she advised. "He said he wouldn't be coming by train, there isn't a convenient one, it seems. He said he'd borrowed a car, and," her voice softened and she seemed to the girl to be hovering protectively over her, "he won't be able to stay very long. It appears he and Sir Alistair have something booked for tomorrow, although he didn't say what it was."

"Probably something to do with that new technique, whatever it is, Dr. Maitland was talking about," Molly said. "You know how it is! People like Flint—and, I suppose, Sir Alistair—get very involved with their work, especially when it's in connection with something new."

"I do know, love," Joan said comfortably. "It's a fortunate thing they do, or where would the rest of the human race be by this time? No further than the first surgical ideas, I'll be bound. He'll come when he can, I'm sure. So eat up your meal and pretty yourself up ready for his arrival!"

Remembering Joan's words, hours afterwards, Molly felt wearily that she need not have bothered. She had done as Joan had suggested, and, to her own surprise, made an excellent meal. Joan had helped her wash and to tidy her hair, as Ann was out somewhere helping Tim and his men. Joan left her a few minutes later, powdering her nose and adding a hint of blusher—something she seldom did—to offset the unusual pallor of her complexion. She had just applied a fresh coat of lipstick when Joan's head popped round the door again, and she was smiling.

"I think your young man's here, love," she began. "There's a super sort of car turning in at the driveway."

She was gone before Molly could collect her wits sufficiently to say Flint's car was by no means a 'super sort of car', but a few moments later Joan was ushering Flint into the room. He looked even larger than Molly remembered him, and twice as grave. He barely smiled, and although she waited for him to kiss her, Molly almost giggled aloud as she realised Flint wouldn't dream of doing any such thing while Joan was around. Evidently the same thought had occurred to Joan, for with a discreet 'I'll bring some tea in later, love. Call if you want it sooner than in half an hour,' she disappeared.

Molly lifted her head and waited for Flint to stoop and to kiss her, but when he did he looked so uncomfortable that she longed to say 'Relax, Flint! They know we're engaged, and they won't be shocked if they do happen to see you kissing me! That's what they'll expect you to do!' But as he briefly deposited a chill kiss on her forehead and then seated himself in the low armchair by the window and away from the bedside, where he might at least have been able to hold her hand, she felt a chilling conviction something was wrong, terribly, frighteningly wrong, and she didn't know what it might be.

"Everything going all right in Edinburgh, Flint?" she

asked nervously, as she waited in vain for him to open the conversation. He cleared his throat, nervously, then reached for a cigarette, something he only normally did when under stress.

"In Edinburgh?" he echoed vaguely, as though he had only just heard of the place. "Oh, yes, thanks. Everything's going ... fine. I ... we're leaving there in October, though."

"After you've left Tunby General, you mean?" Molly tried to sound knowledgeable and sure of herself, but the panic was already rising and she had the dreadful thought that at any moment she might burst into tears. She tried the old dodge taught to her years ago by a sympathetic staff nurse, to open her eyes to their widest extent and so prevent the tears spilling over.

"Yes," Flint said, tapping his cigarette needlessly. "Sir Alistair has asked me to go with him to Switzerland in October. He's opening a new clinic there. I'm to be ... a sort of junior partner."

"That's marvellous!" she enthused, genuinely pleased for him. They had thought it would be years before he could acquire sufficient capital to do anything like this! "What have you used for cash?" she queried. "Charm ... or an overdraft from the bank?"

"Neither," Flint said, suddenly stern. "Lie quietly, Molly. Don't upset yourself, but hear me out. I've something to tell you, something you're not going to like, I don't think, but it has to be said, and I don't want you to blame me too much."

In the silence which followed his words the electric clock on the wall gave a sudden jump of its mechanism and began to give off a curious *ker-plunk* sound as though to mark the passing of each succeeding second. It was a waste of time, Molly thought dully. She was certain every one of those seconds would be etched on her heart for ever.

"You knew Sir Alistair has a daughter, don't you?" he began at length. "Fiona. She's nineteen, and rather a spoiled child, I'm afraid," but he didn't look as though he minded particularly, Molly thought indignantly. There was a very indulgent smile creeping round the corners of his mouth, the sort of smile she had never received from him all the time she had known him.

"Well?" she said at last, her lips feeling suddenly dry.

"It's a difficult thing to put into words," he said, toying with his cigarette in a way which almost drove her frantic. "She ... Fiona, that is," again what she was beginning to think of as 'that silly smile', "seems to have made up her mind she wants me to work with her father—and I can't tell you how much he indulges her! Apparently this started when his wife died, and somehow he poured the whole of his affections on to the girl. Sir Alistair asked me if I'd like to join him, and of course I was enthusiastic. It's just what I've dreamed of ... but not this way, only there was no avoiding the issue."

"You mean ... Fiona's part of the ... the bargain," Molly said, keeping the note of hysteria from her voice with some difficulty. Only the sudden anger she felt saved her from the indignity of weeping out loud, that and the fact that Flint—the wonderful, god-like Flint she had adored for so long—looked as uncomfortable as a first-year houseman, caught out in some breach of hospital rules.

"Don't put it like that," he said with distasteful anger, reverting to what she now saw was always his line of defence when things did not go according to his own plans. "It isn't like that at all! Fiona's a nice child, she's educated. She's been acting as hostess for her father for years. She knows who is who and just how to ... carry off something as important as the opening of such a clinic. She knows who to encourage, and whom to send about his business. ..."

"And so you'd like your ring back, wouldn't you?" Molly finished for him, feeling she could bear to listen to nothing more. "I'm one of those it would be ... advisable to ... send about her business, so," she tugged desperately at the small circlet of gold and diamonds of which she had been so proud. "Here you are."

She held it out to him, letting it lie on the palm of her hand, not touching it. Flint made no effort to take it. He rose and towered above her, looking as uncomfortable as Molly hoped he was feeling.

"I ... don't want it, thank you," he said briefly. "Keep it, as a souvenir. You'll meet someone else ... forget me. I just had to do this, Molly. You do see, don't you, that it would be madness to throw such an opportunity away? It may never come my way again, or not for years and after more hard work than either of us can imagine right now. This is handed to me on a plate. Raise yourself up, if you can. That Aston Martin's an engagement present from Sir Alistair to us both, he was so pleased. ..."

"So pleased you were sensible enough to get rid of me," Molly flared, "or doesn't he even know I exist?" she demanded.

"He knows we've been good friends," Flint was beginning. He had decided on the spur of the moment that it would be as well not to let her know Sir Alistair had believed Molly was a distant relative of Flint's and that he had promised her mother to 'keep an eye on her' while her parents were abroad.

"Friends!" All the dreams she had dreamed, all the ideals she had built up seemed to Molly to be crashing about her ears with some actual physical violence. Suddenly she could not bear the light weight of the ring on her palm another second.

"Here, take it!" She thrust her hand out as far as she could reach, and when he made no movement to accept the ring she clenched her fingers and, using all the force she could muster from her almost prone position, she threw it across the room as hard as she could.

"I'm ... Molly, I'm sorry...." he was beginning, but he made no move towards her, and suddenly all she wanted was for him to go, to get as far from Bronton and all its associations as he possibly could. Foolishly, perhaps, she felt while he remained anywhere close to Beckside Farm he was, in some unknown manner, contaminating the very atmosphere, an atmosphere which, she realised through her tears, had been absolutely ideal until that dreadful day when she had ridden Satan against the advice of everyone who knew the horse.

"It's not his fault!" she stormed into her pillow as, dimly she heard the sound of the big car starting up outside. "It's not Satan's fault, or mine. It's ... Flint. This would have happened even if I'd gone to that seaside boarding house. He'd only to meet someone like this ... Fiona, who knows how to act as hostess to someone like Sir Alistair and how to meet with and treat all the important people who'll be a daily part of Flint's life from now onwards."

Joan had seen Flint's precipitate departure from her home and, after hesitating a moment, opened the door of the 'office' and looked in on the girl. She was wise enough not to say anything at once. In her heart Joan knew this wasn't the sobbing of a brokenhearted girl, but

35

the angry tears of a woman whose pride was hurt, but nothing more. She seated herself beside the bed and gently stroked the girl's hair where it lay on the pillow, not speaking.

After a few moments Molly's sobs ceased, and she lifted a tear-stained face to smile a watery smile at the older woman.

"I'm sorry," she managed, gulping down a noisy sob rather as a child might have done. "I . . . don't make a habit of going off like that!"

"Perhaps you don't make a habit of choosing your . . . intimate friends with due care, either, love," Joan said quietly. "That young man would look well on a television commercial, advertising some natty type of suiting, but I don't think he'd wear as well as worsted! Don't waste any more tears on him, lovey. He's not worth it. And if whatever's happened is because he thinks you're going to be a cripple or anything, then it's up to the Mobile Unit to prove him wrong, isn't it? And, with your help, they'll do exactly that!"

"It isn't. . . ." Molly stopped. It would salvage her pride if she could pretend that was what had happened, but she couldn't be less than honest where Joan and her family were concerned.

"It isn't quite like that, I'm afraid," she began quietly. "This would have happened, even if I hadn't had an accident. He's found someone else, someone who can really help him in the way he needs to be helped. Sir Alistair Grahame's daughter . . . and they have her father's blessing!"

"I bet they wouldn't have if he'd known Dr. Cardew was engaged to you!" Joan said firmly. "I've met him once, it's a few years ago now, but he came as specialist to a case of mine and he was a charming man, and I would have said he'd very high principles. I'm sure he would never have encouraged...anything if he'd known Dr. Cardew had a fiancée already! You're well rid of him, love, and don't forget that! No man worth his salt would go behind his fiancée's back in that fashion, let me tell you! I believe a person's word should be their bond, unless circumstances are *very* much against their keeping their given word. The right thing for him to have done was to have written first, or at least told Ann when she phoned him."

"He wouldn't feel able to do that," Molly said wearily. "He won't want anyone to know. You won't say anything, will you?" she pressed anxiously. "Not even to Ann?"

"Not if you don't want me to do so," Joan promised. "If and when you do, let me know. There might well be all sorts of gossip otherwise, and gossip in a small place is apt to get a little out of hand. Now," she moved briskly, seeing the girl's eyes were dry again and that she was more or less in control of her emotions again, "let's have that tea together. I'm glad Dr. Cardew didn't stay for any now! I'd have felt like putting something nasty into *his* cup!"

"Be careful where you tread, Mrs. Flecker," Molly said quietly. "I'm afraid...the ring Flint gave me's somewhere on the floor. I don't want it particularly. In fact I'd like to send it back to him by registered post if we can find it. I'd better not do that," she continued talking, almost to herself. "If Fiona sees it she'll...think things, begin to be suspicious, and I wouldn't want to be the one to spoil things for them now!"

"You're just what Ann said of you when she first wrote about you, lovey." Joan stopped and picked up the ring which her keen eyes had already seen glinting from under the bookcase where it had finally come to rest.

"I'll lock it away," she said quietly. "If you decide what you want to do with it, you've only to say. Now for that cuppa!"

She was back within minutes, beaming.

"Another visitor to cheer you up, I think," she said pleasantly. "Dr. Maitland's car's just come up the drive. He always welcomes a cup of tea. Must have smelled my brewing up!" She laughed her cheery laughter as she departed, and Molly could hear her calling from the kitchen.

"Molly's in the office, Doctor. I'm just making a cup of tea. Go right in, I'll be with you in two shakes!"

Abruptly Molly was conscious of her reddened eyes and the slight tremble of her lips—something she didn't seem able to control at the moment—but if John Maitland saw anything in the least unusual about his patient, he didn't give any sign. He took her pulse, hummed a little, then took a more intent look at her.

"Fretting?" he asked lightly. "Try not to, Nurse. It isn't easy for someone who's always been active to have to lie up like this, especially when the sun's shining and everyone else appears to be having the time of his or her life! I often think," he said, suddenly serious, "that everyone reaches this point at some time or another of their lives. It's as though one has been *too* busy, perhaps too busy to really think, or to note the natural beauties and delights that lie about us everywhere! I have the curious feeling that, if we refuse to allow ourselves to pause, either to think or to relax, then either we become ill or happen some accident, such as you have done, which forces us to rest for a while : gives us time to think."

"You . . . it sounds reasonable," Molly said grudgingly.

"I'm afraid I'd only looked on this as a sort of punishment for not taking heed of what was said about Satan!"

"I don't believe things work out like that," John said with positive assurance. "I believe there are rules—not exactly rules, but something like that—laid down for all of us, from the word go."

"Shakespeare put it rather better," Molly's spirits were already lifting, he was so matter-of-fact and yet so friendly. That was the word, she decided. "He said, or at least I think he was the one who said it, 'There is a destiny that shapes our ends, rough-hew them how we will.' That's what you mean, Doctor, isn't it?"

"I couldn't have put it as well myself," John laughed, digging into his pocket and producing a battered-looking pipe. "Do you mind?" he asked, packing it with extreme care.

"Of course not," Molly smiled, and suddenly realised that a few minutes ago she had thought she would never smile again, at least not at any man! "I think I'll join you," she went on. "I don't often smoke, so my cigarettes aren't handy. If you wouldn't mind . . . they're in that handbag over there."

He handed the bag to her, waited until she had selected a cigarette and applied a match. They were smoking companionably enough when Joan Flecker came in a few moments later, pushing a laden tea-waggon in front of herself.

"Date cake," she announced, and Molly laughed aloud as John's eyes gleamed when his hostess handed him a thick wedge.

"You spoil me, Mrs. Flecker!" he said, but he was smiling as he turned to Molly again. "Every time I come here," he explained, "I'm presented with my favourite cup of beverage, made exactly as I like it, and either date cake or a delicious concoction Mrs. Flecker calls 'home-spun', though why, I'll never know! It's the best fruit cake I've ever eaten, and I've been given samples of quite a few in my time!"

"I call it 'home-spun'," Joan said quietly, "because it's made from a recipe of my grandmother's which she thought up herself during World War One. Ingredients were scarce, and she invented this sort of baked pudding-mix, I suppose it was really, and we all like it."

"You ought to take out a patent or something," John laughed. "They don't make 'home-made' cakes like that any more."

"Then we'll have to bake one especially for your next visit," Joan told him. "Another slice?"

He was so boyish in his enthusiasm that Molly found some of his quiet gaiety infectious, and they were all three laughing and talking happily together long before the tea-pot was emptied.

"That was delicious," John said as he drained his cup for the second time, then he glanced at the clock on the wall, checked his watch and rose.

"I'll have to give you a run-over, Nurse," he said, "but I really think you're making excellent progress. If you'll try to relax a little, and not feel so resentful of what has happened! It might have been a great deal worse, you know, and this isn't anything but what a good rest and care won't cure, in time."

"Time's the factor, Doctor," Molly said quickly. "I want to be *doing* something as soon as possible! I can't lie here, day after day, as though I were some sort of incurable, or as though there isn't some useful thing I might be doing with all this time!"

"Such as?" his eyes were twinkling. "What else are

you good at besides your nursing, and I've first-hand reports there's nothing wrong with *that*!"

Molly didn't even wonder from whom he'd received these reports or what they had to do with her case history. She was too busy answering his first question.

"I did take a commercial course, before I decided what I really wanted to do was to be a nurse," she said slowly. "It's years since I did any typing, or shorthand, for that matter. But I wasn't bad at either. I managed my first certificates in them both, anyway, but," she gestured vaguely at her prone form, "that isn't going to do me much good either, is it?" she said ruefully. "Not lying here like this."

"It might do you a great deal of good in a few weeks' time," Dr. Maitland said briskly. "You do realise you won't be able to work on a ward for some months, don't you? And I can quite see your point about not wanting to be 'stuffed into admin.', was your expression, I believe?"

"Not in Tunby General, anyhow," Molly said decidedly. "I know someone who went into admin., for light duties for six months. That was two years ago, and she's still there, aching to get back on the wards, but no one will hear of it!"

"I wasn't thinking of Tunby General," Dr. Maitland said quietly.

Joan began to stack the tea-things and to push the trolley away from the room.

"We're forming a group central practice," he said when Joan had left them. "There are five of us, all doing work in the various small townships and villages around here. Two of my intending partners are already in partnership at Bronton-by-Water, and the other two are partners in Bronton-on-Tor. I'm the odd man out," he grinned, so that she knew he didn't mind this at all. "Bronton itself has only ever had one doctor at a time, and just now that's me," he said emphatically if ungrammatically. "I know each of the partnerships has a secretary-cum-nurse, and I've already asked Mrs. Flecker if she'll do a daily stint on my behalf, and she's most kindly agreed. But she couldn't tackle the paper work, and these days," he sighed, "there's such a lot of that sort of thing. I wonder," he smiled on her with that engaging smile she was finding it hard to resist, "if you'd at least consider giving it a trial run while you're recovering? You can always tell me the moment you think you'll soon be fit for ward duty again, and give me time to look round for someone to replace you in the work?"

"If . . . you're not just saying this because you're trying to make a niche for me, are you?" Molly demanded, hating herself for even suggesting such a thing. She wouldn't have even thought of anything like that but for the way in which Flint—whom she had trusted—had treated her. He shook his head.

"Ask Mrs. Flecker—Nurse Joan, as everyone calls her even now—if you don't believe me!" he said emphatically. "She knows all about the group central practice, and she knows too that the one thing which was worrying me was the prospect of having to beg some of the others to allow *their* secretaries-cum-resident nurses to handle mine as well as their own! I'd love you to come." He glanced at the desk calendar on the bureau opposite. "If the Mobile Unit begin work on you next week," he planned aloud, "by September—at any rate by the middle of the month—you should be able to manage a sedentary job while you grow stronger and," he smiled again, boyishly, "while I advertise for someone to replace you. Not," he concluded despondently, "that I have much hope of success around here!"

"May I . . . do you have to have an answer just this minute?"

"Of course not!" John said emphatically. "You'll require time to think this over, my dear. The Mobile Unit will be along during the coming week, I'll arrange that. I'll be round again a week from today and see how you're faring. Once we get you going we can always have a twice weekly session at the new hydro-therapy pool we've all managed to get going out at Bronton-by-Water. I'm a great believer in hydro-therapy, you know, although in your case, thank goodness, I don't think there'll be very much resulting paralysis! I hope you realise just how fortunate you've been, young lady! If Satan had rolled on you, I tremble to think what might have happened."

"Don't think about it," Molly shuddered, suddenly envisaging what the results of such a catastrophe might have been. "I won't, I assure you. I only know it was equally fortunate that Billy Fox saw Satan bolt, and that," she smiled at John, "you have such a good hospital and medical service in Bronton!"

"You're in good hands with Joan, anyhow." John prepared to leave. "By the way, when does Ann go back on duty?" he added as Mrs. Flecker returned.

"Next week," Joan told him. "We shall all miss her, and I expect Molly'll miss her more than the rest of us put together! They've been good friends since they met at Tunby General, and going back on duty, leaving Molly here like this, won't be pleasant for either of them."

"Couldn't be helped," John shrugged, "and, as I'm afraid I keep repeating, it might very well have been a great deal worse! Count your blessings, was what my grandmother always used to say to me when I moaned, and it's advice I never tire of passing on to my patients! Be seeing you, Nurse!" he ended cheerily, and, followed by Joan, who saw him out, he left the house.

Joan was back almost immediately, bustling about the place as though inspired by some new impulse. Never able to remain silent for long together, she burst into chatter long before John's car could have got further than the end of the lane.

"We're all sorry about what's happened, lovey," she said briskly, "but, as Doctor says, it might have been a great deal worse. I expect I'm being a very selfish woman, but," her smile belied the words; no one, Molly thought, watching the way it lit up her whole attractive face, could ever accuse Joan Flecker of being selfish, "but with you remaining here it won't seem so bad when Ann goes back. I know she has to go, and I knew all about that when she wanted to go to Tunby to nurse instead of going to the Cottage. All the same, whenever she's been home for any length of time it seems the place is empty without her, and I'm kind of lost, if you know what I mean? Having Tim and the men to look after's an ordinary matter. It's when Ann is home I manage to add all the niceties of cooking, planning extra treats and so on I never even think of when she's away. Now I shall be able to carry on just as though you really were the second daughter I've come to thinking of you as being, and I hope you don't mind . . . no reflection on your own parents and home, lovey!" she concluded as though anxious not to give offence to any feelings Molly might have had on the subject.

"I'm grateful, Mrs. Flecker," the girl said sincerely. "I've written to Mum and Dad and told them not to worry, how good you've all been to me, and that I'm in the very best of hands here! I expect you'll be hearing from them any day now, to thank you."

"I've heard," Joan said, blushing. "I didn't mention it because I thought they were *too* grateful in their thanks and praise. It's only what they'd have done for Ann if the circumstances had been the other way around, I'm certain. And," the blush deepened, "we've all grown fond of you—for your own sake. You do know that, don't you, love?"

Suddenly embarrassed, Molly muttered something she hoped sounded reasonable, but she was pleased when, at that moment, someone knocked on the door and Joan was called away.

If Joan had meant what Molly *thought* she was hinting, then she couldn't stay here at Beckside Farm for much longer. Tim had been most attentive since she had been brought back to the farm. Tired though he was when he had finished the work of the day, he would leap to his feet if he even thought Molly required something, and she didn't delude herself that it was all only to save his mother the extra work having an invalid in the house entailed.

"He's neither said nor done anything to give me ideas," she reminded herself, "but somehow I've a feeling ... and I don't want another so-called love affair .. not for a long time! What I've had with Flint's been more than enough for me! I'll try to have a word with Ann to drop a hint before she goes back," but even as she made the resolve she knew in her heart it would be difficult to say any such thing to her friend.

Ann had never really liked Flint Cardew. She had— and apparently quite rightly—believed him to be a snob and a social climber as well as a clever doctor. On the other hand she adored her brother, and Molly knew only too well that a match between her best friend and her beloved Tim would be welcomed by Ann with open arms.

She was still wondering how she could phrase her feelings to Ann when the tablets John had left for her took effect and she drifted into slumber, her problem unsolved.

CHAPTER TWO

UNTIL Ann's departure, back to Tunby General and to duty, Tim behaved exactly as he had done ever since Molly's arrival at Beckside Farm.

He was attentive and helpful, joking with her in a friendly way, bringing in anything which he thought might interest her when she became housebound. A new magazine, going to the mobile library on her behalf after first taking the trouble to find out from Ann just what sort of reading matter appealed to her friend.

He arrived home one day scarcely concealing his excitement, and over the tea-table announced his latest addition to Molly's comfort to the entire household.

"I saw Pam Barton in town this morning," he beamed round on everyone. "She's home for a holiday, and I persuaded her to come in and give Molly a hair-do. I know," he grinned at the invalid in an unabashed manner, "how much you girls set store by such things, and Pam went to some fabulously expensive salon in London to finish her training as a hair stylist or something. She said she'd be delighted. She even," he gave his sister a mischievous grin, "said she'd do yours for you. Anyhow, she's coming this evening, so I hope neither of you mind!"

"I don't *mind*!" Ann announced in such a curt tone that Molly wondered what sort of girl Pam was to bring such an alien note into her friend's normally pleasantly friendly tones. "It's just that it seems such a waste, so far as I'm concerned. Had you forgotten that after tomorrow my hair'll have to be practically hidden under my cap, brother dear?"

"I had, as a matter of fact," Tim said, suddenly sobered, "but never mind," brightening immediately. "Pam said she'd do them both for old times' sake and because your mother was so good to Gran, so I guess it'll give you a thrill to arrive back at Tunby looking like a million dollars, whether Matron appeciates the effect or not!"

"I'm grateful," Molly said unexpectedly. She felt she *had* to say something to make Tim feel his efforts hadn't been completely wasted, although this was something she would never have thought of for herself. Tim had looked so dashed when Ann had made her curt announcement, and Molly suddenly felt that was unfair when apparently all he had been trying to do was to think of something which would please both Ann and her friend.

"But I don't honestly see how she'll manage," she began, but Tim, confidence restored, laughed heartily.

"She's got some equipment here," he announced. "D'you remember, Mum, how she was going to start her own business in Bronton and then she won that competition and was off to London before she'd even started here?"

"I remember," Joan said dryly. "And she wasn't regretful, either! Not that I blame her," she added hastily, forestalling any unfavourable comment Ann might have been about to make. "It was a wonderful opportunity, and it appears she's made the most of it."

"By all accounts she's done that all right," Ann said, still ungraciously. "She didn't think Mick Haslett was good enough for her, once she had the chance to go to London! Since then I've heard she's never without an escort—a different one every week, so far as I can make out—you'll see how she'll end!" she concluded darkly. "And Mick's still keeping his chin up and saying she'll come back one day, when she's had enough of the bright lights, I don't think!"

"I still don't see. . . ." Molly wasn't allowed to say more. Tim brought his chair over to sit beside her, and picked up the note-pad which had been lying on the bed-cover.

"I fix up the small table here," he sketched rapidly, showing a small table behind Molly's bedhead. "I connect the long hose from the shower . . . so," his pencil flew. "You let your head—and your hair—hang back. Pam washes it, your hair, I mean, rinses it, sets it in some fantastic style which'll make you feel like a film star, and then sets up her mobile hair drier. You'll have your own private hair do by a top-notcher, and without anything more than one of Mum's famous cuppas and a piece of 'home-spun', a good gossip and that's all there is to it! I thought you'd both be pleased!" he concluded in an aggrieved tone.

Reluctantly Ann admitted that she was rather taken with the idea, 'if Pam's less egotistical than she used to be,' and Molly joined her a little more enthusiastically than she would have done had she not felt it unkind of Ann to dampen her brother's enthusiasm so well.

Pam arrived about an hour later, and while she could admire the girl's precise treatment of her hair, and the skill she showed, the wonderful understanding of the best way to bring out her own best features in spite of the restriction of her unusual position, Molly could well understand the warmhearted Ann's thinly disguised hostility to the entire affair.

Pam was an unusual-looking girl—not pretty, not beautiful, but with an indefinite attraction which seemed

49

peculiarly all her own. The evening was almost ended, both girls looked, as Joan said, 'fit for a queen,' before Molly realised just what it was Ann so obviously resented, and which she herself felt although until this moment she hadn't been able to pin-point what it was.

Pam was *condescending*. There was no other word to describe her attitude. It was as though, without saying a word to that effect, she was intent upon impressing upon the two girls the fact that she was doing them a favour. It wasn't, Molly decided, as though either girl would have asked her to do their hair. It had simply been, she could see quite clearly, that Tim, in his masculine lack of knowledge of such matters, had thought this would be a good idea, cheer Molly up and, perhaps, help heal whatever breach—for it was apparent there had been one—existed between his sister and the girl who had left for life in the city.

If that had indeed been his hope, it was already doomed to disappointment. Molly would have liked to have been more fulsome in her thanks, but Ann so evidently resented Pam's attitude that her acknowledgement that she looked 'special' was tempered by the quick reminder that 'Matron won't think so,' and in consequence Molly could only add a quiet 'thank you very much. It *feels* better, too. I was beginning to feel the need of a hair-wash at any rate,' which didn't seem very adequate.

When Pam had left Tim came into the office and immediately began to complain of Ann's behaviour.

"You knew how I felt about her," Ann retorted. "When we all went to school together you and Mick were always friends, and I'd have thought you had more loyalty to your friend than to make a fuss of the girl who did her best to wreck his life!"

"I say!" Tim protested quickly. "That's a bit much, isnt it? I'm fond enough of old Mick, you know that, but if his girl-friend had decided to go it alone for a time, that was none of my business! You know yourself that loving someone doesn't necessarily mean you make them love you! That's the thing about love, it seems to me," he added wisely. "You can't command it, you can't beg for it. You can only do your best to please, and accept the results, whatever they might be! Mick's had a rough deal, I grant you. He ought to try finding someone else to take Pam's place, instead of mooning about—when he's not flogging himself to death with work—and looking as though the end of the world is due any moment!"

"If it had happened to you . . . ." Ann was beginning, but at that moment the telephone rang, and Joan called from the kitchen to ask one of them to answer for her. Ann, being nearer to the door, went off in a flurry, leaving a scowling Tim alone with Molly.

The scowls cleared as though by magic as he seated himself beside her bed. His glance roved appreciatively over her changed appearance, and the scowl changed to a smile.

"That new style suits you," he said, after a moment. "If you return to Tunby General looking like that you'll have all the medical staff—and some of your patients—wanting to date you," and then, as though aware that he had made an error in mentioning the medical staff of Tunby, he began hastily to talk of how pleasant it had been since her arrival at Beckside.

"I'm glad you're not going back yet," he said in conclusion. "I expect you'll have to spend some time convalescing, don't you call it? Where better to do that than here, where Mum can look after you and where we'll all do everything we can. . . ."

"That was Sister O.P. from the Cottage," Ann came in, interrupting her brother's speech. "The Mobile Unit will be here in the morning, about eleven o'clock. Sister said they couldn't give the time more precisely, and she knew we'd understand. It will, of course, depend on how many other cases they have and how long each treatment takes."

"I know," Molly agreed, but Ann carried on talking. "Dr. Maitland suggests they take you into the Cottage and he puts a back slab on for you as extra support," she said. "Afterwards, when you're partly mobile again, I expect they'll replace it with a light surgical corset."

"I expect so," Molly sighed. "Seems I've let myself in for quite something, not taking Satan's temperament seriously."

They talked lightly about varying cases similar to Molly's which either or both of them had known, then Ann went off back to her room to complete her packing. Tim offered Molly a cigarette, and when they were both smoking he said abruptly, and in a much quieter tone :

"I said I'm glad you're not going back yet, Molly, and I meant it. In fact," he seemed suddenly awkward, "I'd be pleased if you decided never to go back at all."

Deliberately Molly pretended to misunderstand his meaning. She drew deeply on the cigarette and stared up at the ceiling.

"I must," she said briefly. "It's my work ... and it's what I want to do. All my interests and my friends— except your family, now I've met you all—are in Tunby. Nursing's what I've been trained to do, and that's what I want to go on doing, so there we are."

"You can nurse just as well in Bronton, dear," Tim said briefly, then Joan bustled in with a plate of freshly baked tarts and the inevitable tea-pot and cups. Tim made an irritable gesture, and Molly's eyes twinkled as she caught a muttered something about 'this place being as private as a main line railway station,' but her temporary amusement faded as she noted the sullen look which had clouded Tim's handsome face.

She had seen that sort of look on Ann's face on more than one occasion, and it never boded well for anyone. It always meant Ann had set her mind on some course or other, regardless of authority or of anything else. If Tim was possessed of the same brand of tenacity and if, as she suspected, he thought he had fallen in love with her, it was going to be more than difficult to rid him of that illusion—for she was certain that was what it was—while she remained at Beckside.

The conversation became general and remained so throughout the evening, and although Tim did his best to be the one to linger in the office after supper, Joan firmly marshalled them all ahead of her, as only someone with her years of training and experience could do, and he had to leave along with the rest of the family.

Molly lay awake a long time after everyone else had gone upstairs to bed. She couldn't stay here the weary weeks it would take for her treatment to become effective. On the other hand, where could she go, and to whom? She knew no one else in the village, and the Cottage was full. Perhaps, after all, she ought to remain at Beckside Farm until the treatment was completed. Then, when she was somewhat mobile and had a job to go to—which seemed already arranged—she would have to look for somewhere else to live. She would make the excuse that it was too far from the village to the farm to make her staying there a practical matter, and if Tim—as she suspected he would do—suggested driving her to and fro she would have to rely on her own powers of persuasion about the work which lay ahead of him, to influence him into accepting her decision.

The first and most important thing was the matter of the Mobile Therapy Unit. She liked the staff nurse in charge immediately, and there was no problem and surprisingly little discomfort about the back slab. It was arranged that the Unit should visit her twice each week, and that once each week someone from O.P. would call and take her to the hydro-therapy pool, to speed her recovery, as Staff Lawson smiled.

Certainly Ann's return to duty went off, as Joan said, without a hitch, even though she'd gone back without her 'partner in crime'! it being a standing joke with Joan that where her daughter was there was always bound to be something happening, although this time the 'happening' had not been even remotely funny and only Molly had been involved!

"I'll let you have all the news," Ann promised. "And I'll give your love to Sister Baxter!" which called forth hoots of laughter from both girls until Molly explained that Sister Baxter was always prophesying dire things happening to her nurses, and now she would be certain her warnings were fully justified!

"I'll be down on my first forty-eight," Ann promised, and then she was off, sitting beside Tim in the station waggon which he had brought round for that purpose.

"I have to pick up some things at the station," he had said, teasingly. "Might as well do the two jobs at one and the same time. Saves petrol!"

Afterwards Molly always looked back on the night of Ann's return to Tunby as marking yet another period in her life. From the time when he returned from the station, having seen his sister on to the train, it seemed Tim was determined to spend every available moment in

Molly's company, until the girl was sure his work must be suffering and that Joan would begin to dream dreams Molly was by no means certain could ever be fulfilled.

August drifted to a close in a flurry of wind, heavy showers and thunderstorms.

"Serves everyone right for switching the Bank Holiday nearly into autumn!" Joan said, watching the rain pattering on the window.

"Only one thing wrong with that sentiment, Mum," Tim said from his customary position close to Molly's bedside. "The powers-that-be fix the holiday! They don't normally have their own holidays at the same time as the rest of us, and anyway, you can't hold them responsible for the state of the weather!"

"I don't remember Bank Holidays like this when I was a student," Joan persisted, as stubbornly, Molly thought in amusement, as either of her children. "Summer was summer, before the last war! *And* we knew where we were with winter! It's all this outer space, flying to the moon and to the other planets and what-have-you that's causing all his weather upheaval! Nobody'll ever convince me otherwise!"

"Nobody who knows you would try," Tim said lazily. "But let me remind you of something, Mum. You once said if ever we heard you talking about 'the good old days' to remind you that you used to say that was a sign of growing old! And you're not showing any other signs of doing that, so I'd stop it at once, if I were you!"

"It's true, though." Joan was persistent, but Tim only laughed.

"Look in the records for the past twenty, thirty, forty years," he suggested. "There's always been peculiar weather, at all times of the year, and someone's always had an explanation for the freak storm, the drought or the flood, which ever happened to be the cause of trouble at the time. No," he was suddenly sober in speech and manner, "the weather's always been the same, with variations, if you get me. No one can tell from one year to the next, and never will, it seems to me. It's like love." He was suddenly, Molly felt, putting more meaning into his words than the words themselves implied.

"I think there's something in the Bible about 'the way of a man with a maid', and that hasn't changed either, has it, Molly? There's still the same attraction, the same . . . dangers, the same thrills, don't you agree?"

"I don't know." Molly's tone was more curt than she was aware until she noticed Joan's startled look and realised it was her manner which had occasioned that glance, half of enquiry.

"I'm off love for the time being," she affirmed with more vehemence than was necessary. "And I have a feeling I shall take a great deal of coaxing to change my mind . . . if I ever do !"

"Because it still hurts, lovey?" Joan's tone was gentle in the extreme which, paradoxical though it might be, was perhaps the cause of the pricking of the tears behind Molly's eyelids.

"Not in the way you might think," she admitted honestly. "I think I always knew it wouldn't work. Flint was so . . . so far above me. Not only professionally, I don't mean. He lived in a different world, even if that was only—then—in his imagination. I think he always knew where he was going, and that he'd get there. I think he will, and good luck to him. It wasn't until he said that about Fiona Grahame being 'educated' and knowing how to deal with . . . with the kind of people

Flint will be dealing with from now onwards that I recognised how wide was the gulf between us."

"Gulfs may be bridged," Joan said quietly, but Molly shook her head.

"That one would never be bridged," she said firmly. "Neither of us had anything strong enough with which to build the bridge. I can see that now, but," she was abruptly on the defensive, "that doesn't mean I'm ready to try again ... not yet!" she said in such an assertive tone that Joan knew it would be useless to attempt to talk her round to any other point of view.

"In that case," she rose, turning down the light and tucking the covers more firmly about her guest, "don't let yourself be stampeded, not even by Tim, much as I love him. It might," she added on a thoughtful note, "be as well if you could find somewhere in the village where you could live, once you're working at the surgery. I don't want to lose you, goodness knows. I love having you here too much to send you away, and Ann will be very cross if she thinks I've even put such an idea into your head."

"It was there earlier this evening," Molly admitted. She had found it easy to talk to Joan from the moment they had met. Now she was more grateful than ever for the older woman's understanding heart.

"I know only too well how stubbornly persistent my family can be, Molly," she said with a wry smile. "It's something they've both inherited from me ... the elder boy didn't have it, but he's abroad now."

"It would be kinder to think of it as tenacity," Molly smiled. "My mother always says that's a good characteristic to have, in the right place."

"One has to be certain it *is* in the right place first, though," Joan was still thoughtful. "I'd love you as a

57

daughter-in-law, and I'm not going to deny that! Yet an unwilling or uncertain daughter-in-law would be, ultimately, of no use to Tim, to me or even to herself. I think you'll have to get away from Beckside, to see this whole situation in perspective. Wait until you're ready to go to work for Dr. Maitland. I can ask him then if he knows of anyone in the village where you'd be all right. He's sure to know someone. He knows everyone and their entanglements around the whole of Bronton, and he'll realise it will be best for you to be near to the surgery and to the doctor's house. Leave it for the present...and I'll try to see Tim understands you're not to be worried just yet."

"I can manage, but thanks all the same," Molly smiled, and said good-night. It was of strange comfort to realise that Tim's mother loved her, but, at the same time, was prepared to put her ultimate happiness before Tim's obvious desires.

She was thinking over the conversation as she fell asleep, and, to her own surprise, found the next morning that she had, perhaps subconsciously, decided it was Joan's long experience of human nature, the fears and the glories as well as the frailties which beset the entire human race, which had given her that unexpected understanding of her visitor's problem.

What his mother said to Tim, Molly never learned, but after that brief talk with Joan there were no more sentences with hidden meanings, no hints that her prolonged stay at Bronton would mean everything in the world to Tim.

He was as attentive as ever, as anxious for her well-being as he had been since her accident, but there was a hint of reserve in his approach now, and some of the dancing lightness had gone from his eyes, his voice and his general approach where Molly was concerned.

When, about mid-September, Dr. Maitland pronounced her well enough to begin her new work and at the same time suggested—quite casually—that it might be better for saving Tim's time and for taking some of the burden from Joan, if she went to stay with Miss Spofforth, a small, frail elderly spinster who lived in Rosewood Cottage, two or three cottages away from the doctor's house, Tim remained silent.

At Joan's suggestion he took Molly's cases and the trunk which Ann had had sent on from the Nurses' Home at Tunby, down to Rosewood Cottage, and when Joan also suggested she accompanied Molly to her new lodging to see her settled in, he still made no objection.

As he carried her small trunk inside and upstairs Molly felt suddenly guilty and turned to Joan, about to burst into impulsive speech. Joan, with her acute understanding of people, had apparently sensed something of what she was about to say, for without saying a word she laid gentle, restraining fingers across Molly's lips.

"Leave it, lovey," she said quietly. "Sort yourself out first. Tim will be a good friend. Whether or not he becomes someone dearer than that we'll have to wait and see, but don't act on an impulse you'll regret later. That way comes only unhappiness for you both . . . and for the rest of us. Wait!"

Tim came down then, and Molly could hear him talking with Miss Spofforth in the tiny kitchen. His deep voice and the light, cracked tones of the elderly lady mingled for a moment or so, then Tim's deep laugh rang out, with the lighter note of Miss Spofforth's joining in.

"Tim's heart's undamaged as yet!" Joan said seriously. "He'll not be hurt, not beyond his pride, by your coming here. Don't forget, love, we want you to come and see us whenever you like. And if Tim gets ideas and they don't coincide with yours, tell him so. He'll perhaps make a scene, but he won't hold it against you as much as if you tried to deceive him, and failed. That he'd never forgive, so, unless you do find you love him—and I mean love—send him packing. He'll thank you—and respect you for it—when he's had time to think!"

There wasn't time for more. Tim, whistling as though he hadn't a care in the world, returned followed by her new landlady. Joan kissed her before she left, and Tim reminded them both that they were not more than a few miles away, then he helped his mother back into the station waggon and they drove off, leaving Molly feeling strangely bereft.

CHAPTER THREE

THERE wasn't much time to feel either lonely or bereft once she had settled into her new surroundings. Miss Spofforth's cottage was very small after the vast rooms of the old farmhouse, with its unexpected corridors and little rooms opening off here and there and used for all manner of things, from the storing of old furniture and farm equipment to the rows of apples on their racks.

Rosewood Cottage, on the other hand, was small, neat and compact. As its owner said on more than one occasion, she had to have a place for everything and have everything in its place, or she would be totally swamped by what she called 'clutter'.

Certainly there was nothing untidy, nothing useless in the small, neat homestead. The brasses shone, the furniture gleamed, and the curtains and the linen were spotlessly white. Bowls of flowers and pot plants were everywhere, and in all the drawers were sachets of lavender which Miss Spofforth picked and dried from her own lavender hedge and then sewed meticulously into small muslin bags.

She was as enchanted to have Molly's company as Molly was to be there. The tortoiseshell cat which slept by night in a basket beside his mistress's bed and spent the day either on the wide window seat or in the pretty garden accepted Molly as equably as did his owner, a fact which pleased the old lady enormously.

"Cat's a great judge of character," she announced as Cat wound himself, purring, round Molly's feet. "If he hadn't accepted you, I might have had to change my mind," she said with surprising seriousness. "Doctor said he would, though, and he was right. Those old Egyptians didn't make their cats into kind of gods for nothing, though. They know more than we give them credit for. Cats, I mean. And I always rely on Cat's judgement."

Amused and pleased by the fact that Cat had obviously accepted her, Molly prepared to settle down for an evening's chit-chat about the village and 'the good old days', but she was pleasantly surprised to discover that her new landlady had, apparently, been only awaiting the arrival of someone to whom she could talk in what she termed 'my own language'. That 'language', Molly soon discovered, was a love of poetry and of history, both of which were the very breath of life to the old woman who had once taught in the village school and dreamed of what she could—and would—have done had she been fortunate enough to have been born in a later generation.

"I don't know what you think of all this talk of reincarnation, Nurse," she insisted upon giving Molly her title, although the girl protested she would rather use her christian name, "but I'm sure I hope there's something in it. I don't want to waste all the things I've learned in nearly seventy-six years of living. I want to use it again, and I don't know how . . . but I believe I shall."

The subject was fascinating, and Miss Spofforth had read a great deal about it. Molly began to feel she could have sat and listened and discussed into the small hours of the morning, but around half past one sleep began to overwhelm her. Her eyelids grew heavy and she had great difficulty in hiding her yawns, despite her interest.

Miss Spofforth stopped abruptly in mid-sentence, and before Molly was aware of it was pouring forth apologies and a cup of creamy cocoa at one and the same time.

"I'm a selfish old woman," she chattered on. "Dr. Maitland will say he did wrong to ask you to come here if you tell him how late I've kept you talking. I shall not apologise for *that*, though! I've been starved for someone to exchange ideas with ever since Miss Hexthorpe retired from the school and went to live with her brother in the Midlands. She and I used to have some really good talks, and none of them gossip or nonsense, you understand! But now you're tired, and you're not really well, and it's all my fault so that if you are late—or sleepy—in the morning on your first day at the surgery, don't hesitate to tell Dr. Maitland to look in on me. I'll explain, and I'll make certain it doesn't happen again. We'll plan our talking time for when you're free and not on morning duty! He'll understand. He's that kind of man. Ought to be married. He's the type to make one of the best husbands in the world, but he doesn't seem interested in that sort of thing at all."

Molly scarcely listened. She smiled, sipped her delicious cocoa—so different and yet so strangely like the cocoa she drank in the ward kitchen on night duty—and went finally and sleepily to the little bedroom with the white-covered bed smelling fragrantly of lavender.

She had slept well all the time she had been at Beckside, except when the pain in her back had been especially bad in the beginning. Now she slept peacefully and dreamlessly through the night, and not once, not even before she fell asleep, did she even think of either Flint or of Tim. Instead she thought vaguely of all the old lady had been saying, and when she fell asleep it was with a faint smile on her lips, a smile which, had she but known it, was the outward sign of the sudden quietude of her innermost thoughts.

Despite the lateness of the hour at which she had

gone to bed she awakened as the sound of Miss Spofforth's alarm penetrated her slumbers. She felt refreshed and ready for the day ahead, even though she did admit to a vague disquiet as to what it might hold.

She need not have worried. She had just managed to fasten the light surgical belt with which she had been fitted since the discarding of her back slab, when Miss Spofforth tapped on her door.

"I've brought you a cup of tea, Nurse," she said as Molly called to her to come in. "I always like one the minute I waken, and I have one of those little alarm things which brew it as it wakens you, so you don't have to worry about my getting up to do it! It's all here, laid on, so to speak. By the time you're down I'll have breakfast ready. It was only a matter of laying out places and amounts for two instead of for one. I've done it this way for years. It saves no end of work and time."

She was quite right. Later Molly learned how the old lady had organised every moment of her time in order to have sufficient leisure to attend to her two favourite recreations, reading and the cultivation of her small but lovely garden, in that order.

While they had talked the previous evening, each trip to the kitchen had contributed in some way to the work of the morning being eased. The rashers of bacon had been laid in the pan. Two eggs cracked and left in cups ready to pop into the hot fat the moment they were needed. Bread had been cut and left under a plate in the tiny gas-fridge. Extra bread had been cut and placed similarly near the toaster. By the time Molly was dressed and downstairs the fragrance of the frying bacon was wafting through the cottage, ousting even the scent of the lavender and flowers.

"Cereals on the table, milk in the fridge," Miss Spofforth said briskly. "I do hope you're not one of those Americanised people who want coffee for breakfast?"

"I'm not really bothered," Molly said, amused. "I do prefer tea, but. . . ."

"Suits me," announced Miss Spofforth briskly. "Nothing like a strong cuppa in the mornings, I always say. And several times a day as well, if you need 'em. I do, and I'm not ashamed to admit it!"

She went to the gate, accompanied by Cat, tail waving like a plume as though in farewell, to see Molly off for the short walk to the surgery.

"Nurse Banstead'll be there," Miss Spofforth said. "She's with the two doctors from the Tor. She's a nice woman, but a bit forbidding. Don't take any heed of her tongue, Nurse. Her bark's worse than her bite!"

"I . . . is she much older than I am?" Molly asked, feeling suddenly foolish, but Miss Spofforth seemed to understand.

"I should think so," she said non-committally. "She was a Sister at the Cottage for years, then she gave up nursing for a time and went to look after her father. I understand she came back to it when he died. Dr. Doyle looked after the old gentleman, and I expect that's how she went to the practice in the first place. She's been with them 'bout two years now, receptionist and all sorts. A good woman, but sharp-tongued at times," she confided. "Not like Nurse Taylor—she's with the others, the ones from Bronton-by-Water. She's a widow from the last war, and never seems to have got over the shock."

Feeling more and more uncertain of what was expected of her, Molly went on to the house which stood back from the road and which had a brass plate outside the door on the left and two others, obviously newly placed there, on the right. A small mahogany notice-board stood in the garden and announced to the world that the Bronton-Group Centre had its headquarters in this house, and the names of each of the five doctors painted in white were inscribed thereon.

Molly walked up the path and through the wide open door. A middle-aged woman in a plain white nylon overall greeted her as she approached what looked like an office reception desk.

"What name, please?" the woman asked pleasantly after greeting her. "Have you an appointment?"

"I . . . I'm not a patient," Molly began almost apologetically. "I'm here as Dr. Maitland's receptionist-nurse."

"Didn't he tell you to come in by the side door, then?" the other asked briskly. "Oh, of course. You're the girl who's been in the accident, aren't you? You won't know the layout of the Doctor's house yet! Unless you've visited?" she shot the last three words at Molly like bullets from a gun, so that in spite of her outward-looking calm the girl flushed, although she could not have said why.

"I've . . . this is the first time I've been here," she began, but almost at once they were interrupted by the arrival of Joan, who at once took control of the situation.

Molly found herself shepherded around the place as though Joan knew every nook and cranny, as indeed she possibly did, for she had often helped Dr. Maitland Senior out when he had needed a nurse on hand, as Molly discovered later.

She was shown the three consulting rooms; the one used by Dr. Maitland was his father's old consulting room, and two rooms which had obviously once been part of the large house's ground-floor reception area had been divided and modernised to make two separate consulting rooms for each of the other two partnerships.

"One doctor from each of the dual partnerships is on duty at once," Joan explained. "Dr. Maitland's both an M.R.C.S. and an L.R.C.P. and so he has to allow one of the others to deputise for him until he finds a partner for himself ... which he isn't likely to do, in my opinion, so he works on a self-imposed rota system which seems to work out quite well, but leaves him exhausted sometimes."

Nurse Taylor arrived then, followed almost immediately by the first of the medical men. Nurse Taylor was a tall, angular woman with a very sad face, and Molly felt at once she knew just what Miss Spofforth had meant when she said she had 'never got over the shock'.

Molly was a little worried as she smiled at the other woman. She had never been any good, she thought illogically, when confronted by obvious grief which ran too deep for words.

She need not have given the matter a thought. Betty Taylor's smile deepened and she lifted the flap of the counter-like reception desk, motioning Molly to her side.

"You're the nurse who was staying at Beckside and had the misfortune to have an accident with a horse, aren't you?" she said in a low, melodious voice which came unexpectedly from such a strained countenance.

"That's right," Molly nodded. "I'm Molly Watson."

"I don't suppose you've ever done anything like this before," Betty Taylor continued. "Don't worry, none of us had until a few months ago when Dr. Maitland proposed this scheme. So far it seems to be working well, but it'll work even better now that he's got someone to look after his calls and appointments."

She showed Molly into the small room which the four

nurses shared. There was, Molly was amused to note, the inevitable tea-making equipment standing on a small table adjacent to the sink unit.

"Liz Andrews—she'll be here in a moment or two—looks after the switchboard. Now you're here you'll take calls for Dr. Maitland, of course, do his appointments, his cards, lists and so forth. Liz—we're both Elizabeth, of course, but I'm always Betty and she's Liz to save confusion—worked at the G.P.O. telephones until she was riding pillion on someone's motor-bike and came a cropper. She was off work a long time, and when she heard Dr. Maitland was contemplating this group centre she asked for the switchboard position the next time she came to see him. I must admit she does it awfully well. Takes a lot of work from the rest of us."

It didn't take long for Molly to make friends with her fellow workers. Naturally a friendly, outgoing person, she was delighted to find that, once she was accepted, both Betty Taylor and Olive Banstead were as friendly as was Joan.

Liz, on arrival, proved to be an equally friendly girl of about twenty-two; small and a little too plump for her height, she had an open, beaming face and almost fell over herself in an effort to please. Before the end of the week she was literally following Molly about whenever the telephone didn't ring—which, as it happened, was so frequently that long conversations were impossible.

"I think all nurses are wonderful," the girl sighed one morning when Molly was just beginning to get the hang of it all, to use Betty's phrase. "If I hadn't always fainted at the sight of blood, and if I hadn't known you've such an awful lot to learn and to remember before you can even pass your first exams, I'd have gone in for nursing myself. It might have done something for me," she

68

sighed. "At least I'd have had the glamour of a uniform I was entitled to wear! I don't know why you don't all wear your proper uniforms all the time, with cuffs and caps and whatever it is that tells people you're all staff nurses! I would, if I could."

"No real nurse goes into the profession for the glamour of the uniform, Liz," Molly said. She felt she was sounding suspiciously like Matron, but she *had* to say something! "I suspect your ideas of nursing have been coloured by the films you've seen, the books you've read, but it isn't really like that at all!"

"I saw a picture once," Liz began dreamily, "and the young nurse was in the theatre for the first time. She fainted!" she said dramatically, "and the young surgeon she'd fallen in love with carried her out and looked after her. They were married by the end of the film," she concluded with a heart-felt sigh. Molly laughed.

"And in real life," she said, suddenly sobered by the memory of Flint and his treatment of her, "the young surgeon wouldn't have taken the slightest notice of her if she'd fainted directly at his feet, much less *touch* her, when he was all scrubbed up and germ-free and about to perform even a simple operation! No, Liz, my dear, hospital life isn't like that. . . ."

The telephone shrilled and she had to break off in mid-sentence, but when they paused for their mid-morning break, and when, according to the leaflets which had been sent round to all the patients, only emergency calls should be coming in, Liz returned to the subject. It was very plain that she had an idealised picture of life in any hospital, and equally plain that neither Betty nor Olive had succeeded in making her see how far from the truth was the picture she had made for herself.

"I didn't know I wanted to be a nurse when I first left school," Molly told the girl. Being nearer to her own age-group she had the feeling, whether rightly or wrongly, that Liz might listen to her and take note of what she had to say.

"I took a secretarial course," she went on. "One night, when I was coming home from work, there was a bus accident. I wasn't involved, fortunately, but I was upset because there wasn't anything I could do to help the people who were, and who were in pain and who had to wait for someone to help them."

There was a long pause, and Liz waited, not speaking.

"When the ambulance arrived," Molly went on, seeing again in her mind's eye the scene as it had presented itself to her on that night, "I saw the two nurses who accompanied it and the ambulance men. *They* knew what to do and how to do it! They knew the right way to move the injured people without hurting them further, and when the ambulance drove away I knew they—or other girls like them—would be in charge of these people, and in their hands lay a good percentage of whether or not the injured ones would recover. It was then I gave up my job and decided to do something which I knew would be useful and welcome anywhere in the world."

"But it *is* glamorous, isn't it, Molly, really?" Liz persisted, and Molly, meeting Betty's glance, smiled.

"In one way, yes," she said steadily. "There's the glamour, if that's the right word, of knowing you're helping. There's the glamour—again, if that's the right word—of the uniform, although at first it takes some time to get accustomed to it and to changing it quickly whenever it's necessary. There's the thrill of knowing that in obeying the instructions of the physician and the surgeon you are helping another human being back from the well of pain and the loneliness it brings. In brief, it's the glamour of thinking whenever you see someone who needs your help 'how can I help you? what can I do for you, to ease your pain?' and somehow," she wasn't aware of the change in her tone, but Betty was, and Olive was looking at her with a new respect while Joan's eyes glistened as she nodded approval at hearing someone else put into words the feelings she herself had cherished for years. "It sounds very smug," she laughed self-consciously, "but it's true—it is for me, anyhow, and I'm not special—that it's the spirit of service which gives the profession the glamour. It somehow grows to be a part of your very being. I wouldn't want to do any other kind of work now," she made an irritable movement in the direction of the office. "I shall be only too thankful when I've finished here and I'm back on the wards again!"

"I don't understand, yet in some strange way I do," Liz said in confusion. "I'll have to think about it all a great deal more before I've finally reached a conclusion! But the books and the pictures make it all seem so different!" she ended defensively.

Molly laughed, and the others smiled.

"They don't show you the sluice room, or when a nurse has done her best, given out of herself to the last degree, and then it's... all been in vain," she said soberly. "That wouldn't be good for the glamour image, but it would be a sight nearer the truth! You think about it a great deal more, Liz. And if there's anything else you want to know, I'll do my best to help if I can. But it's the sort of life you have to try for yourself. Not everyone's cut out for it, you know, no matter what they say about it being instinctive for a woman to want to help nurse anyone and everyone!"

71

"Do you," Liz began, and then hesitated to continue after a moment, "think like this about the patients who come here?" she asked curiously. "What about Mr. Germain, for instance?"

"I don't know him," Molly said. "Should I?"

"You will," Liz nodded firmly. "He rang this morning and I expect you've made the appointment for this afternoon, but you won't perhaps remember the name. He needs a dressing on his hand."

"What about him?" Molly asked, seeing Olive glance at her watch and realising it was time to close the surgery except for the one who was to remain on call.

"He's a retired journalist," Liz said succinctly. "Goodness knows how old he is, but he's clever, though you wouldn't think it to look at him. He's scruffy—there's no other word for it! He says he's going blind, and that I can well believe, but he's not too blind to see those horrible little traps for the mice in his house instead of getting a cat, like your Miss Spofforth! Anyway, it was setting a trap that caused the accident to his hand, and the injury's gone the wrong way or something. Serves him right in my opinion!" she ended with the devastating candour of youth. "Mum says it'll handicap him in his work. He's writing a book or something about his years on the *Bronton Globe*. Mum says he'll have unearthed some real old scandals, she wouldn't wonder, and if that's so, I'm not sorry for him one little bit!"

"No spirit of service there, Liz," Molly teased, but the girl merely shrugged, unrepentantly.

"You'll see," she said darkly. "He's not a nice man. He wouldn't set traps if he were, would he?"

"I think you'd better find out the conditions of an animal nurse," Molly teased, but as Betty and Olive were ready to leave—and Joan had already gone—there wasn't time for more discussion just then.

"You have something about being back on the ward, Molly," Olive said as she changed into her outdoor things. "I often wish I were back, but they practically asked me to leave the Cottage to make room for the younger end. I'm glad to have this job. At least it keeps one in touch."

Betty made no comment. She didn't say whether the work at the Centre was enough for her or not. Her mouth tightened into the same sad lines, and she quickly pulled on her small hat and with a muttered 'see you both in the morning', was on her way, her little three-wheeled car tut-tutting down the road.

Molly walked, slowly and thoughtfully, the brief journey to Rosewood Cottage. Strange, she reflected, how so many illusions had grown up around the profession she loved. They were understandable illusions, but one had to give the life a trial before one knew whether or not one could ... settle.

She was thinking of a girl who had been in P.T.I. with her and who had held the same delusions as did Liz. It hadn't taken long, not even to the end of her first year, before she knew she would never last out the whole of her training, let alone a lifetime in the profession.

"It might not be the same for Liz," she reflected as she pushed open the gate and was greeted by Cat purring round her feet. "I hope she'll talk some more about it. Good nurses—the ones who really want to nurse—ought to be encouraged, but not those who think it's a short cut to either soothing a fevered brow and hooking a wealthy patient or running around in circles where the medical staff are concerned, and ending with their illusions—and hearts—shattered!"

She pulled her wandering thoughts together as she went into the kitchen and greeted her landlady. She never thought about Flint now, and she didn't intend to do so, if she could help it. He was part of the past. He had chosen the way himself. Let it remain as he had chosen. Molly just didn't want to know, she assured herself.

She listened as Miss Spofforth recited a passage from Keats which had enthralled her that morning. As she listened to the words *'At the tip-top there hangs by unseen film an orbed drop of light, and that is love'*, her eyes misted with tears.

Since she had come to live in Rosewood Cottage it was amazing how quickly she had rediscovered the power of words, the way in which they could touch the heart, bring tears of joy or sorrow, depending on the mood. Before she had become enraptured with Flint she had been a great reader. Now she was amazed to find that her reawakened love of books, of words, brought more comfort than she would have ever believed possible. How could she have so neglected that first love of hers, and especially, she thought with self-scorn, for someone whose mind was on such mundane matters of fame, glory and finance to the exclusion of all else, even of honour!

Thinking along these lines she was reminded of Liz's words about Mr. Germain. Without being a gossip in any sense of the word, Miss Spofforth knew almost all there was to know about everyone in Bronton, Bronton-by-Water and Bronton-on-Tor. Thinking of this now, Molly asked casually:

"By the way, we've a patient coming in this afternoon for a dressing, a Mr. Germain. Liz seems to have something against him because he won't keep a cat!" She was laughing as she spoke, but there was no answering laughter in Miss Spofforth's reply.

"Alex Germain?" she said on a questioning note. "Be careful of him, my dear! Once he knows you have some free time and haven't a boy-friend or whatever one's young man is called these days, he'll be out to exploit you, one way or another! He's the meanest man in three countries, and I'm not joking. He wouldn't give a blind man a light! He's worth a fortune, most of it made from raking up all sorts of stories that would have been better never told! Just you beware, love, and if he wants you to do anything for him, and he'll ask, I know, be sure you have an agreement, a watertight agreement, and that all the benefits are on your side! He'd get more than blood from a stone! He'd get living tissue!"

Molly had never seen Miss Spofforth so upset, and, wondering what the poor man had done to have her speak of him in this way, she hastened to change the subject.

"I don't suppose I shall have much to do with him," she opined. "Just see him when he comes in and then show him in to Joan to do the dressing, that's all. What *is* that delectable smell?" she queried, and in a moment, as she had known she would do, Miss Spofforth was well and truly launched on the subject of the intricacies of the tempting meal she had prepared and which was now simmering on the stove, ready to eat.

CHAPTER FOUR

THE hours of the group centre were set but vastly differing from those of a normal private practice, which had been Molly's sole experience in dealing with this type of work.

Before eight-thirty in the morning, a patient could call his own particular doctor at his home, and on his normal phone number. From eight-thirty, all five doctors' telephones were put through the centre number, and it was Liz's task to switch them through to the respective doctors.

Appointments for the day had to be made by phone before ten-thirty in each morning. Appointment times—for Dr. Maitland, at any rate—ranged from nine each morning until twelve o'clock. Alternate afternoons they ranged from three to five or four o'clock until six in the evening. Unless previously arranged he saw no patient in the surgery after that time, but Molly knew, via Betty, that he did a great deal of evening visiting to patients too ill to come to the surgery and who had neither phone nor neighbour to arrange to call for them.

Alex Germain's appointment was for half past four, it being one of the days when John would be at the surgery until six o'clock in the evening, what Liz laughingly called 'late turn'.

There was a Mrs. Barnes preceding him, and she had brought her son with her. The child had been 'helping' on his father's farm and fallen, cutting himself badly. The cut had been stitched and was progressing very well, but, as she would have expected of him, John was keeping a special lookout over the boy, despite the injections against the dreadful tetanus.

She watched Mrs. Barnes and Ralph depart, the latter's cheek bulging and she smiled to herself, remembering how Dr. Maitland kept a jar of what he termed 'goodies for good children' to whom he presented one or the other of the varied contents of the jar. Evidently Ralph had presented no difficulties, and went out contentedly munching.

John's buzzer sounded, and after a glance at her list to see who was his next patient, Molly went along to the waiting room and asked for Mr. Germain.

The elderly man she had noted sitting in a corner seat of the waiting room, rose to his feet. He was terribly thin, his nose sharp and his eyes bright and gimlet-like under bushy brows. He clutched his well cut though ancient topcoat about him as he followed Molly along the corridor to the door labelled 'Dr. Maitland'. Just before he tapped on the door the buzzer sounded again, a different note this time, and Dr. Doyle's voice could be heard asking for Mr. Crouch.

"Why doesn't young Maitland use that inter-com system?" demanded Mr. Germain in a truculent tone. "It would save you a great deal of extra walking about, young lady!"

"Dr. Maitland thinks the personal touch of greater importance, I believe," Molly flushed. "Anyhow, I don't mind."

A disgruntled 'humph' was the only response, and a moment later the door had closed behind him and the little orange light appeared above the door indicating John had a patient with him.

Molly went back to her lists on her desk, checking

through the remaining appointments. She knew Mr. Germain would be passed from Dr. Maitland through to the room where Joan would attend to his dressing, a task John Maitland wouldn't hear of herself undertaking until she was, as he put it, a great deal stronger.

She was rapidly typing some lists of drugs John required, when she was aware of rather than saw, someone standing before her desk. She looked up, anxious to help if she could, and saw to her astonishment Alex Germain was facing her, a scowl on his lined face.

"Yes?" Molly queried politely. "Can I help you, Mr. Germain? You should have gone out through the side door, you know," she added as an afterthought, wondering if, in some unaccountable way, he had lost his sense of direction since the exit was clearly marked.

"I know, and through the so-called kitchen garden," the old man said in a disagreeable tone. "I heard you typing, though. Heard too many typists not to be able to recognise the touch of an expert when I hear it!" he went on. "Wanted to talk to you."

"I can't talk just now, you know," Molly said, rising as the buzzer went for John's next patient. "I'm supposed to be working here," she smiled to rob the words of any implied rebuke, "not gossiping."

"It was about work I wanted to talk to you," he said uncompromisingly. "You're wasted here, you know! You should be in an office, earning good money as someone's secretary, or doing some work on your own account. Anyhow, you could do better than this, and I can put you in the way of it."

"Not now, please!" Molly said urgently as the buzzer went again and—imaginative though it might have been—she felt there was an undertone of impatience behind its summons.

"Come and see me at my house, then," he thrust forward a slightly grubby card with his name and address and telephone number printed on it. "You'll find it well worth your while. What time do you leave this place?"

"About half-past six," Molly said, the urgency of the buzzer making her more abrupt than was her wont. "I go home—to Miss Spofforth's, that is—for my dinner then."

"And in the evening? Waste your time watching the soap opera stuff on the television, I suppose!" he sneered.

Molly flushed. Both his tone and the seemingly hidden meaning behind his words annoyed her. With an effort she controlled herself and held back the sharp retort which had trembled on her lips.

"Not very often," she said. "Look," as the buzzer became imperative, "I'll pop up and see you this evening. I'll ring first to see if it's all right. I can't stay to talk any more now . . . excuse me!"

She was kept busy right to the moment when the last patient had gone and Liz, Joan and the other nurse on duty—tonight it was Olive—and herself had finished tidying up so that everything was in readiness for the arrival of Mrs. Briggs, the daily help.

Molly was just pulling on her coat when John came out of his consulting room, and as soon as he saw her he came briskly across to confront her.

"Just a moment, Molly," he began in his customary pleasant, friendly tone. "What happened between Germain's leaving and Ivor Jones coming in? I deliberately didn't ring for anyone else until I knew Joan had finished with him. He can be a very funny customer when he's in the mood and I waited until I was sure he'd gone."

"You mean you waited until you thought he ought to have gone," Molly's eyes were twinkling. "He wasn't . . . awkward, exactly, but he did come back here and tried to talk all the time you were buzzing for Mr. Jones. I'm sorry," she apologised belatedly, but Dr. Maitland smiled.

"Don't apologise," he said briefly, frowning. "I ought to have guessed something like that had happened and come out and sent him packing myself! What did he want?"

"He wants someone to do some typing for him, I think," Molly said, suddenly worried. "I'm not quite sure *what* he wants, but that seemed to me to be the gist of the matter. I'm not interested, of course!" she hastened to add, "but I do have a great deal of free time, you know, and if I *can* help him. . . ."

"If you're wise you'll soon realise the less you have to do with him the better for you," John Maitland said abruptly. "It's not my business—as yet—but if ever anyone needed psychiatric help, that man does. He's a menace the way he is. I'd strongly advise you to have nothing further to do with him, Molly. And I'm serious about this!"

"I'll have to go and see him tonight," Molly said unhappily. "I sort of promised. I needn't do any work for him, of course. . . ."

"You're a free agent, of course." Did she imagine it or was his tone more formal than usual? "I just advise you not to have anything to do with him. He's a warped mind, and in my opinion he needs skilled attention. There's a good psychiatric clinic at Farrowby. If I could get him in there they'd soon sort him out, and he'd be a useful member of the community again. Just now he's what I said . . . a menace."

"He didn't seem very menacing to me," Molly smiled, not because she was amused but because suddenly John appeared to be taking the whole thing far too seriously.

"It won't hurt me to find out just what it is he wants, and then either tell him I'm not interested, or suggest where he might find the help he needs."

"Suit yourself, of course." John picked up his bag as a sign the interview, so far as he was concerned, was at an end. "I'm just telling you what my opinion of the man is, that's all."

Molly went back to Rosewood Cottage in a dismal frame of mind. No one, it appeared, had any sympathy for the elderly journalist, and as always everything in her called out to her to champion the underdog.

Miss Spofforth, when consulted, was little comfort. She briskly stirred the beef and rice dish she was concocting and spoke without turning round.

"That man's no good to you or to anyone else, Nurse!" she said crisply. "Dr. John's right, he needs some kind of treatment, but so far he hasn't done anything to merit anyone sending for help. It's all done in such an underhand way, if you know what I mean? He's a nasty mind, and if he wants to publish all the scandals—and there are some, I can tell you—he's unearthed in his years around this area, I don't see how we can prevent him, short of putting him under restraint. It doesn't seem to occur to him that when the poet wrote 'the pen is mightier than the sword', he was meaning that one should use the pen in a good way, as one should use a sword to defend the right, only now, I suppose," she smiled and sighed, "it would be a sawn-off shotgun or something of that nature. I suppose in time it'll come to a 'space or ray' gun!" she ended so gloomily that Molly laughed aloud.

"So far as I can be certain," she said, "I understand Mr. Germain uses a typewriter—or did, until he injured his hand."

"He could have borrowed Cat," Miss Spofforth said crisply, adding almost at once, "if Cat would have stayed with him, which I doubt. There's no need to worry about *him*," she said emphatically. "He's lived alone all his life—so have I, for that matter—but he's alone in spirit as well, if you get my meaning. He's no time for humanity, and one day he'll be sorry for that!"

Molly couldn't argue, as she didn't know the man well enough, but she did know he hadn't a friend, or so it seemed, and for that reason alone she felt she must keep her promise and see what it was he wanted of her.

Miss Spofforth tut-tutted, but in vain. Molly hated to be the cause of her landlady's disapproval, but this time she felt there was no help for it. She had made a promise, and she would keep it. So far she wasn't committed to anything; there was still plenty of time to make up her mind, and to change it if she wanted to do so.

She would have been utterly astonished if she had known someone else was also worrying about her visit to Alex Germain's house. John Maitland had completed his visits for the evening, with the exception of one which he made as regularly as time would allow. He had returned home tired, but more than that, troubled. His housekeeper, who had kept house in his latter years for John's father, took one look at his tired features when she carried in the sherry with which he liked to relax before his evening meal, and sighed.

"Just like his dad," Alice Burton told the stove as she turned the small roast and put the heat down a shade. "Someone—or something—has got him by the heart again. It isn't right for a man who cares so much for people's pain to be a doctor! It tears too much out of them."

Alice would have been completely astounded had she realised it wasn't someone's pain which was upsetting John. Indeed, he turned his glass in his hand as he thought, he himself didn't know quite what it was. Somehow this newly acquired assistant of his... bothered him. There was no other word for it, for she didn't bother him in any particular way as someone with a serious illness or accident would have done.

"She worries me," he admitted to himself, yet she was making a perfect recovery from the accident. He himself had seen to it that she had a job which gave her independence and yet which didn't put too great a strain on her until she was well enough to cope with more. Then what was it?

He paced the floor of the room which had been his father's favourite one and in which he, John, liked to relax and to sense the old gentleman's helpful presence around him. No woman, he reminded himself, had bothered him since Elaine. Elaine! Even now, although it had all been over and done with years ago, just after he'd entered the practice, the memory of her cool, dark beauty had the power to bring her image to life in his mind. Nothing more, he knew that. It wouldn't have been at all the right thing to have continued with their engagement, but all the same, it was comforting to remind himself that neither her memory or her image, nor that of anyone else, had given him any emotional trouble until the arrival of this little quiet nurse at Beckside Farm.

"I scarcely know the girl," he reminded himself. "For all I know she might just be the kind to revel in the dirt old Germain seems to enjoy ferreting out from goodness knows where!" but he knew instinctively that Molly was the kind of girl to shrink from even reading the stories the old man would enjoy churning out in the hope of finding a publisher who felt there would be commercial value in scandal!

Why hadn't he had the sense to have asked her if she would like to do something interesting in her spare time? There was enough work for both of them—and for more volunteers—in the self-imposed task of looking after the inmates of the two homes for displaced persons which a kindly authority had permitted to take over two of the old, large houses in the area.

Not all the inmates came under the one heading. Some were in a land alien to them and their ways. Some had been here since the war ended, others—mostly youthful relatives of those already there—had been brought to join them or to live in the second home nearby. All of them had one thing in common, they were in desperate need of human kindness and sympathy, as well as of more practical forms of help!

"And while there are wars, upheavals, even natural upheavals like earthquakes and floods," John thought, "there'll always be a need for places like these and for people to run them! There's work a-plenty for willing hands, without going to old Germain's and doing his mental scavenging for him. It's no business of mine, but...."

There lay the crux of his problem. It *was* no business of his, but his concern made it so. He didn't want to know Molly Watson was having anything to do with someone like old Alex Germain, who, if he had avoided the drink which had finally cost him his job before he had been due to retire, had been an able enough journalist with a flair for news and a real sense of a story in even the most mundane of happenings.

"Something must have warped his sense of proportion

84

years ago," John thought now, nodding absently as Mrs. Burton signified his dinner was being placed on the table. "That's beside the point—he can get help, if he will. But Molly would be appalled ... it was when I read that first draft of his when he brought it along to ask me if he'd got the conditions of the typhoid epidemic right. I felt I'd been handling dirt ... and Molly would react that way, I know. And as she's so sensitive it'd go deep. And she's just been hurt enough, I think."

He thought about it all the time he was enjoying the excellent meal Mrs. Burton had prepared. Afterwards, when he had been out to a patient on the moors nearby, he sat quietly before the dying embers of the fire Mrs. Burton always insisted upon lighting from the first evening in September onwards, and thought again.

Perhaps she wouldn't want his kind of work, although not for one minute did he imagine she was offering to help Alex Germain purely from a financial angle. She was paid at a higher rate at the centre than she had been receiving at Tunby General, but that, John was certain, did not influence her in any way, and the moment she was pronounced well enough to go back on to the wards, he was certain she would leave.

If the reason wasn't financial, as he was certain it wasn't, and he was equally certain even Molly's tender heart hadn't as yet been deeply touched by the shambling, shabby-looking figure of old Germain, only one valid reason remained.

She wanted more work because her hours were brief, the work was comparatively light, and after the busy life of a staff nurse in a large hospital in one of the new over-spill zones, he felt she perhaps imagined she was wasting some time. To waste time, for the kind of person he instinctively felt her to be, would be the height of wicked folly. He could be right, he could be wrong, he concluded, as finally he put out the lights, all save the lamp above the door which had burned showing the Doctor's House ever since his great-grandfather had started up in practice there, over a hundred years ago now. Morning, and Molly's reactions to Alex Germain and whatever it was he wanted her to do, would, he hoped, give him the answer and enable him to help.

He wasn't quite prepared, despite all his thought, for his answer when he was given it by a pale-faced Molly with troubled eyes. She asked to see him when the last patient with a morning appointment had left. Although they both knew he was due to go to one of the outlying villages almost at once, he invited her to bring her coffee into the consulting room, and once settled comfortably, asked in what way he might be of service.

"That's it," Molly said unexpectedly. "Being of service, I mean. That man who came yesterday to have his hand dressed—the retired journalist—asked me to go to his house last night and see if I would like to help him with a book he's writing. He wanted me to do the typing for him."

"And?" John prompted, as she hesitated.

"I can't," she said quietly, after some minutes. "It isn't that I can't do the work, it isn't that I'm not sorry for him and feel someone ought to help him. It's . . . oh," she made a little face of sheer distaste, "I don't know how to explain it, but he read me two chapters of what he'd written last night, and it was *horrible*! No bad language or dirt or anything to which one could point a finger, but a sort of . . . insinuation all the way through, if you know what I mean, that the people about whom he was writing were . . . very wicked, and he was going to prove them so. It wasn't in so many words . . ." she floundered helplessly, and again made the futile gesture. "It's so difficult to explain," she concluded simply.

"I'm not surprised," John said, controlling his anger that she should unwittingly have exposed her sensitivity to such a procedeture. "I only scanned his columns when they were in the *Globe*, but I knew one of the sub-editors well, and he often said if they'd left in half what Alex wrote they'd have been sued for slander every week. It isn't so much what he writes as what he leaves out ... and implies. Everyone fills in his or her own version, and all of them aren't either kind or understanding!"

"That's what I felt," Molly said, relieved that he had understood so easily. "I told him I'd think it over, but I'd already made up my mind, and I'd foolishly said I'd a lot of free time and would be glad to help."

"You can overcome that without any trouble at all," John smiled. "I have a scheme too. I do voluntary work for people who aren't in a position to help themselves. Wouldn't you rather come in on something like that, Molly?"

"I'd love to!" she began enthusiastically, then she flushed a very becoming pink as she added with seemingly undue haste : "I don't know what it is you do, but I'm certain it won't be calculated to *hurt* anyone, rather the reverse, I should imagine!"

"That's the intention, anyhow," John said quietly, relieved to find it was going to be, after all, quite easy to explain. "I presume Miss Spofforth is expecting you home for lunch?" he added.

"Yes." Molly smiled. "I'm supposed to be on time ... it's a cheese soufflé and it's important to have it at exactly the right moment!"

"I should think so, indeed!" John agreed heartily. "Mrs. Burton feels the same way, and I appreciate the fact! I'll call for you directly after lunch, then. I'll go out to Mrs. Best now, and pick you up around two o'clock. All right?"

"Fine," Molly said dubiously. "But where are we going? Should I wear uniform?"

"Not unless you especially want to," John smiled. "I would suggest a thick two-piece and jersey, if you have one with you. It's chilly outdoors these days, and part of our afternoon—only a part, mark you—will be spent outdoors."

He said no more, and Molly did not press for an explanation. Something told her he was planning a surprise, and so complete was her trust in his judgement she did not want to spoil things for him by asking needless questions.

"I'll be ready," she promised, rising so that she wouldn't delay him further. "It all sounds very intriguing, but what am I going to tell Mr. Germain?" she worried aloud.

"Leave it to me," John dismissed that problem without further ado. "He doesn't know it, but I'm just waiting until he writes or does one more outrageous thing and then I'll have him in Farrowby Royal Infirmary for observation. I've had my eye on him for some time. He can be restored into being a very useful citizen, and he's certainly got a clever mind. I'm sure with treatment of the right kind he might well turn out some good, reasonable and interesting work. We'll see."

"I hope so," Molly sighed. "He seems ... I should say ... once he must have been both a clever and an interesting man! It all seems such a waste."

"We can't put the world to rights, Molly, much as we'd like to do so," John sighed. "We can only do our best as we see it ... and help where we can. I assure you that if I ever have the opportunity to help Alex Germain, then I shall do it and do it right gladly. As it is," he shrugged and smiled, "Mrs. Best and her latest await my attention! See you at two?"

Molly walked back to Rosewood Cottage feeling a little less disturbed than she had felt when she had gone to work earlier that morning. Then she had, she was willing to admit to herself now, been very disturbed indeed. Thinking the matter over she decided it had not been actually even the words of the typescript which Alex had read to her which she had found so upsetting, but the sneering smile on his face when he had been mouthing the words he had written with such obvious maliciousness.

She shivered slightly, and turned the collar of her coat up a little, but although the late November day was dank and chill, the shiver which had run over her entire body had not been occasioned by atmosphere alone.

"It's the effect that man's work has had on my imagination," she decided. "It's funny how anything like that can produce a really physical effect!"

By a valiant effort she dismissed Alex Germain and his affairs from her mind. Cat came purring to greet her, as he always did, and once she was inside the cottage with its pungent scent of chrysanthemums which stood about the rooms in every available vase Miss Spofforth could find, she had the feeling to which she was rapidly becoming so accustomed. When she came in like this, it was always as though the arms of the little house had placed themselves around her, enfolding her and shielding her from all harm.

"I'll grow what Mum used to call 'fanciful' if I stay here for very long," she told herself, obeying her landlady and going up to wash in preparation for the meal.

Busily setting out the meal, Miss Spofforth chattered on. Molly loved to listen to her. She never discussed the affairs of other people. Her discussions centred around books, plays she had watched on her small television set, or her beloved garden and pot plants. Just now it was her bowl of African violets which was the cause of her anxiety.

"I shall keep them moist and humid," she chattered on, "as I did last year. They'll come up again, you wait and see! You'll still be with me by then, I hope?" She paused in her chatter and looked searchingly at the girl. "Young Flecker was asking the other day if you'd made any plans about leaving yet."

Tim! Molly's heart gave a disturbed leap, but was instantly quiet again. Tim wasn't the man to cause her heart to leap for joy, much as she liked him. She knew she could never love him, and there lay the difference. It wasn't the man himself. It was his farmer's attitude to animal life and life in general. She could still remember how appalled she'd been when she had encountered him, some weeks ago now, on his way to the local slaughter-house with a sheep in the truck, a sheep, she learned to her horror, which had once been the lamb which had gambolled about the kitchen and farmyard when she had first gone to Beckside Farm.

"Can't be helped," Tim had said in what seemed to Molly a casual and unfeeling manner. "Having a lamb about the place, and having it grow into a full-grown sheep with just the same habits, is a bit too much. You remember how he used to go under the table in the kitchen when we were having a snack? He still does. But now he takes the table with him, and he doesn't realise that isn't done!"

"But he's been a pet," Molly had protested, but in vain.

"That was Ann's fault, and Mother's," Tim had declared. "I warned them they wouldn't want him to go when it was time, and that we couldn't keep him in and around the house once he outgrew his lambing days! They wouldn't listen. He ought to have been put out with the rest of the flock as soon as he could crop grass."

After that he had attempted to turn the conversation on to a more personal note, but Molly couldn't bear to stand and talk, not with the sheep still in the truck and Tim driving.

She became aware that Miss Spofforth was looking at her curiously, and made an effort to pull her scattered thoughts into something like order.

"I'm sorry," she apologised. "I didn't hear what you were saying. I was thinking...."

"I only asked if you *had* made any plans to stay or to go," the old lady said patiently. "I hope you'll stay a long time, until you're ready to leave and go to your own home, wherever that might be. But it's no business of mine, I realise that! It's just," she paused, and the thin, faded cheeks were stained with a strangely reluctant flush, "I don't know a great deal about life as people understand it, but I've read a great deal and I've observed a great deal more. If you wanted to talk to someone—apart from Tim's mother, whom I know you love—I'd be more than willing to try and help if I could." She made a little twisting movement with her hands, a gesture which wrung Molly's heart.

"I expect you think I'm both foolish and presumptuous," she said at length, "but I've grown very fond of you, Nurse. I've never had anyone to grow fond of since the end of the war, and I'd like you to know that."

"Thank you for telling me," Molly was touched to the depths of her being. Impulsively she moved forward and kissed the spinster on her cheek, surprising herself as much as she had surprised Miss Spofforth. "I've only one problem at the moment," she confided. "I'm going with Dr. Maitland to some mysterious voluntary work of his, and I don't know quite what I've let myself in for! I'm certain it won't be anything like my proposed help to Mr. Germain, but. . . ."

"It'll be the work he does at the two Peace Havens," Miss Spofforth seemed completely *au fait* with whatever it was. "They're two homes which were started just after the war," she explained. "The people in them are all either from concentration camps or camps for displaced persons, or refugees from Czechoslovakia or Hungary."

"I've read of something like this," Molly said aloud. "Are these the same thing?"

"Similar to the ones you've read of, I expect," Miss Spofforth was briskly stacking the dishes as they talked. "I expect there are several such homes all over the country, and all staffed mainly by voluntary workers. They do have some staff, of course, but they work mainly for what one of them called 'peanuts', although I don't think that's strictly true!"

Behind her glasses her eyes twinkled, and as she talked she was busily packing an odd assortment of things into a large carrier bag, a woolly jumper, some thick stockings, a cardigan, several copies of her favourite weekly paper. On top she placed two of the cakes she had made that morning, announcing: "That's a drop in the ocean, I know, but every little helps, they tell me."

Molly said nothing. She was watching as the elder woman took three small plant-pots from her hiding place under the stairs.

"Tell Matron to bring these into the full light gradually," she said, handling the pots as though their contents were of supreme value. "They're bulbs, and they should be in flower for Christmas. I always think fresh flowers are more valuable then than at any other time, and I know they'll all love them."

Molly took the laden carrier and the box with the three pots, wishing she too had something to contribute. As though able to read her thoughts Miss Spofforth reached for the girl's coat, patting her arm in a companionable way.

"Don't worry, my dear," she said briskly. "You can do what I can't do, give what I'm too old and too useless to give. You can give your sight to help darn the clothes that some of the people send in to the home without first mending them! You can turn the sheets 'sides to middles' as we used to call it, to make them last longer when there's not enough money to buy new ones. You can read to those who can't master reading in our language or help the younger ones to learn to read. You can give nursing skill, and I know all that is done on a voluntary basis. Tim's mother often goes of an evening."

"I'm ashamed of myself!" Molly said softly. "I've never before realised these things were still needed, not after all these years."

"They'll be needed for some time to come," Miss Spofforth said firmly. "Maybe for ever, since mankind doesn't seem to profit by its mistakes. There'll always be people in need, or so it seems to me. The Good Book tells us 'the poor ye have always with you', and in my opinion it doesn't just mean the financially poor. There are the 'poor in spirit', the 'poor in hope', and believe me, some of those poor souls are without any hope whatsoever except for what's done for them at the home and by the people who work there. You're doing a good thing, child. And like all good things, it'll be returned to you in some way which will make for happiness."

It came as a strange sense of relief to hear John's brisk tap-tapping on the door. Somehow Molly felt her emotions were being stirred despite herself, and in a way in which she didn't particularly find comfortable! She ought to have thought of something like this for herself, she found herself deciding, instead of waiting to have the needs of these people pointed out to her by someone she had only known such a short time.

John, apparently, had no such thoughts as he helped her into his car and started out from the village. As he drove he pointed out places of interest, and chatted—not with Alex Germain's maliciousness but with real interest—about the people and the houses as they drove past them. Molly found her interest stimulated and her attention held right to the moment when he turned the car in through widely opened gates and drove up a pathway meticulously weeded to come to a halt at the foot of a flight of stone steps which led to a vast old oaken door.

"Here we are," he announced, jumping out and handing her from her place at the other side, carrying the bulging carrier and leaving Molly to carry the plants. John himself carried a parcel evidently packed by Mrs. Burton, and his doctor's bag as he led the way to the door which he tapped at briskly, before swinging it open and standing on one side for her to precede him.

Molly gazed around shyly, and almost as soon as they were inside a girl of about twenty-five came through a door at the far end of the vast hall, her face alight with pleasure when she saw who their visitor was.

"This is Nurse Watson, Maria," John said slowly and distinctly. "Nurse ... Watson," he repeated, smiling.

"This is Maria," he added to Molly. "Speak slowly and carefully, she's trying hard to learn."

It was the beginning of one of the most fascinating days, or more correctly, afternoons, Molly had ever spent. She was shown the common room, the huge kitchen which, her guide proudly informed her, the inmates had transformed themselves from the neglected place it had been, with its old iron stove and fireplace.

Everything gleamed, and everywhere people were working. One man staggered in with a load of logs which he had evidently sawn for the fire. Someone else followed with coke which he placed carefully amongst the blazing timbers.

At the kitchen table women were stoning fruit, much as, Molly remembered dimly, her grandmother had been wont to do before it was possible to buy the ready-cleaned and washed mixed fruit her mother used when she was at home to save time.

In the common room two women were laboriously stitching at the repair of some curtains which their original owner must have thought too shabby to use and so had sent them on here. Carefully Maria explained how, when they were mended, these would be dyed and look 'so pretty'.

Again and again Molly felt her eyes stinging with unshed tears as she realised how much she had always taken for granted in her daily life, and how much store most of these people set by what seemed of so little value.

"I feel I'll never grumble again," she vowed as, long after they had arrived and when it was almost time for evening appointments, John shepherded her outdoors again.

"Don't feel too badly about having been blessed, Molly," John said firmly. "You have promised to come

95

again—and to come regularly—and to help with any nursing needed. That's a great deal from a first visit. I *like* to come," he added candidly. "It always makes me feel I am paying a little of every man's debt to help wipe off some of the misery of the world. It may be wrong to feel a glow, sort of thing, and perhaps that isn't what one should feel, but I do. Although," he grinned abruptly, and suddenly she realised he had called her by her christian name for the first time since they had met and that she had liked it, "I hope it isn't helping to make me sound a prig !"

"You couldn't sound like a prig," Molly assured him, and was surprised to realise that was the truth. She was liking being with him more than she had ever remembered liking to be with anyone else, even, she realised with a sense of shock, with Flint.

With Flint she had always had the feeling that, try as she might, in some way she was not measuring up to the standards he had mentally set for her. The effect had been depressing in the extreme.

This afternoon, with John—she was already thinking of him as 'John', she realised—she had felt a part of what he was trying to do, and remembering the way in which face after face had lighted up at his approach, she suddenly felt the weight of misery which must have been with the inmates of the home for so long before they had come to safety in its shelter.

"Most of them seem able to speak a little English with a smattering of either French or German," she said quietly as he stopped the car outside Rosewood Cottage. "I used to be quite passably good at languages. I think I'll send for some of those language record things and try to find out how to talk to them better."

"You don't have to send for them," John opened the

door of the car. "I'll lend you mine." He gave a conspiratorial grin. "I had the same problem when I first went to the Home," he confessed. "I sent for the records. They're a marvellous help. I'll bring them round after surgery tonight. You'll find it easier when we visit the children," he continued. "Most of them have learned to talk in our tongue by now, and only lapse into their own languages in moments of stress."

"That's an awful thing," Molly was suddenly passionate. "To lose one's people, to lose one's country must be bad enough. Not to know one's own language as a mother tongue is even worse."

"Don't start getting worked up about it, Molly." John was suddenly serious. "I've noticed this about you on more than one occasion. When we had the woman with the spastic baby for instance. When we had the man so injured by a bull he couldn't ever hope to work or even live normally again unless a miracle happens. It was what was happening to you last night, when you found yourself so sorry for Alex Germain, even though we both know most of his trouble has been caused by himself. Didn't your Matron ever tell you not to allow yourself to get emotionally involved with your patients?" he said in a teasing tone. "Every Matron I've known has made a point of stressing that where her nurses are concerned!"

"I . . . she . . . it's somehow different in hospital," Molly began, but John interrupted quickly.

"It isn't any different all through life, believe me," he said seriously. "If you allow yourself to identify with everyone with whom you come into contact, you'll end by not being sure of who you yourself are or what it is you're striving after, what you ultimately want from life, and that's all wrong!"

"I'm not sure I *know* what I want," Molly was

suddenly as unhappy as she had previously been happy. "I thought I did, now I know I was mistaken ... how does one know when one isn't sure?"

"One knows," John said firmly. "You'll see, but don't allow your heart to be pulled this way and that by the emotions of other people. That way lies self-destruction, and I could see you literally aching to put metaphorical arms about those people, and they wouldn't all have understood your motives."

"I'm not sure I understand them myself!" Molly admitted, a wry smile on her lips. "But I'll remember what you've said. And," she added with a sudden return flash of the impishness which so delighted him on the odd occasions when he had glimpsed it, "if we don't both hurry we'll be late in for your first appointment, and I believe that it's Mrs. Peters tonight!"

John made a face and lifted his hand in salute, before driving the remaining little way to his own gate. He mustn't keep Mrs. Peters waiting, she was a pleasant woman, but felt the dignity of her position as wife of the manager of the only bank in Bronton!

Humming under her breath, her lightheartedness restored, Molly went into the cottage. Miss Spofforth had been watching for her, and before the girl could speak there was a steaming cup of tea and a plate of home-made tarts on the small table beside her.

"You'll need that," the old lady said briefly. "I know it's the night for a long surgery, but don't worry. I've done a casserole and it won't spoil if you're late. By the way," she turned her back so that she was no longer looking into the girl's face, "you've had a visitor," she announced.

"A visitor?" Molly was frankly puzzled, but not left long in doubt as to who the caller might be.

"Young Tim Flecker," Miss Spofforth said quietly. "He came to ask—prepared to beg, if you ask me—if you'd like to spend Christmas with them up at Beckside Farm." She gave what in anyone else would have sounded like a small ladylike snort. "He said if you were worried about leaving me alone," she sniffed, "and I've been alone more Christmases than he's even seen, I was welcome as well. And Cat, though I doubt if he would get along with all the animals they have up there. I said we'd let them know. Did I do right?"

Coming on top of the emotional impact of her visit to the home that afternoon, Molly felt suddenly unable to cope with such a crisis, for that was what the invitation really amounted to, she decided.

Impulsively she turned to Miss Spofforth, and without knowing it there was appeal in the look she turned on the perceptive old lady.

"How do you feel about it?" Molly asked directly. "And what do you usually do at Christmas?"

"There's no 'usually' about it," Miss Spofforth said quietly. "I *always* follow the same programme. I put my Christmas dinner on to cook by itself, so that it's timed to be ready at six o'clock in the evening. I go to church—to the Communion service first, then to the morning service later—once upon a time, before I stopped going out so late at night, I used to go to the midnight service on Christmas Eve. And I used to go to the Watch Night service at New Year. That's by the way, though. That's at the chapel up the lane, as you'll realise," she ended.

"And what else?" Molly persisted. It seemed a bleak sort of prospect to sit alone—save for Cat—and eat her Christmas dinner with no one to share the fun, but Miss Spofforth, as always, had an answer ready.

"Don't laugh!" she admonished, "but at first I used to read *A Christmas Carol* out loud to Cat. He likes it as much as I do," she affirmed, and Molly knew better than to even smile. "Three years ago Mrs. Barrie, the Vicar's wife, died, and I suggested he came back here after morning service and shared my Christmas dinner. He did, and last year and the year before."

"So that if we go to Beckside," Molly said slowly, "that means Mr. Barrie will be alone for *his* Christmas dinner? I know Mrs. Bates only goes into the Vicarage daily."

"I was going to suggest—but only if the idea appeals to you, remember—that you go to Beckside for Christmas Day and Boxing Day—then I suppose the surgery will be closed except for emergency calls for New Year's Day, we can have a little festival all on our own, here, and no one's feelings will be hurt. But don't go at all, if you'd rather not, Molly," she said, for the first time using the girl's christian name and not her professional title. 'Two people in one day,' Molly thought inconsequently. 'Must be an omen of some kind!'

"I think Tim said Ann would be home for Boxing Day," Miss Spofforth continued. "He's making plans to meet the coach, as it appears the trains won't be convenient, but the overnight coach will be running. She would have managed Christmas Eve instead, but she's in the choir or something. Perhaps you'll understand?"

"Perfectly well." A faint, wistful smile touched Molly's lips. "The nurses—those with what Sister Tutor calls a voice—learn certain carols," she explained. "They practise and practise and practise, and it's quite something to watch and listen to them going round all the wards, dressed in their uniforms, capes and all, and carrying a few lanterns. The patients love it, and so do the staff.

Christmas in hospital is quite something, you know! Everyone's so anxious to make up to the patients for their not being home for the festive season, they go out of their way to make life exciting and happy."

"Well," seeing the wistfulness Miss Spofforth dismissed it as briskly as she always dismissed anything negative from her own life, "I daresay there'll be plenty of other Christmases when you'll be there to take part. The thing at the moment, is what are you going to do about Christmas for *this* year?"

Seeing the girl hesitate she spoke again, decisively this time.

"I think you should go to Beckside—if you feel you can," she announced. "If you feel Tim might be ... troublesome, stay here. You're more than welcome, but Ann is your friend, and I thought you'd like to see her and have all the hospital gossip first-hand and so on. I expect Dr. Maitland'll have plans for the two homes as well, and you might be able to help a little there. You're more than welcome to stay here, as I don't think I need tell you, but if you'd like to see Ann and stay with Joan and the rest."

"That's what I think I'll do, then," Molly decided. "I'd like to go to church with you, though, if I may—and if I can persuade someone to bring me to the village."

"That's settled, then," Miss Spofforth seemed satisfied. "And if you don't want a scene with Master Tim when he comes down tonight, as he said he should do to find out whether or not you were going, I should tell Joan, at the surgery, what you've decided."

Molly did a rapid mental check and discovered, to her obvious relief, that this was one of the afternoons when Joan would be at the surgery.

"I'll do that," she finished off her now almost cold tea, "but if I don't get a move on I'll be late for the first appointment, and as Mrs. Peters has the first appointment, Dr. Maitland won't be pleased if I'm late!"

Fortunately Mrs. Peters herself was a little behind schedule and arrived, five minutes after Molly was ensconced in her little sanctum, full of apologies.

"I'd been to have my hair done," she explained without preamble. "I hope I haven't kept the doctor waiting!" she concluded archly.

"Not at all," Molly murmured politely, then as the woman entered the consulting room and the door closed she decided to take a cowardly way out of the difficulty of dealing with Alex Germain and to phone him from the surgery before the next appointment was due to arrive.

It was some minutes before Alex Germain answered the ringing of his telephone, and Molly was on the point of replacing the receiver, feeling sure he had either gone for a walk or fallen asleep, when his gruff, grim voice answered her call.

Following John's instructions, Molly briefly explained that, as she had been unexpectedly asked to help Dr. Maitland with some extra duties she could not fulfil her promise to come and type his manuscript. There was an incredulous silence for some moments, then all at once he began to talk wildly, raising his voice and literally raving into the phone. Molly's heart began to beat faster. She had never been spoken to like this in her life before, and it was most unpleasant. She wanted to put down the receiver, but held on grimly, determined to try and talk some sense into the man before she hung up.

Finally his words slurred into one another, and to her horror she realised John's warning had been true. Alex

Germain's worst enemy was not himself, it was his craving for strong drink, and until he would allow himself to be helped towards a cure, there was nothing anyone could really do to help him.

Unexpectedly she heard the sound of a receiver being replaced, but Alex Germain was still talking, and she realised with some relief that someone else on the surgery switchboard had overheard something of the awful conversation. As tactfully and as quickly as she could she told him someone else was waiting to go in to see Dr. Maitland, and then looked up to find Joan at her door.

"Glad you've got rid of *him*!" Joan said briskly. "If you hadn't managed it, I would have done! I was going to phone home, when I caught your conversation. I wasn't eavesdropping, lovely, just an accident. That man's a menace. He ought to be locked up!"

"He's a sick man, Joan," Molly said worriedly. "Dr. Maitland's right, he needs treatment. I only wish he'd ask for help!"

"Not much chance of *that*!" Joan said emphatically. "He'll have to happen something disastrous before that happens!"

"I'm glad you looked in on me." There was no time like the present for dealing with what had to be dealt with, Molly decided. "Miss Spofforth told me of your kind invitation over Christmas. I was worried about what she would do, all alone, but she seems to have everything already arranged, so, if you really would like me to come, I'd love to be there."

"Good," Joan sounded satisfied. "That'll hold Tim's nattering for a bit, anyway," she grinned suddenly. "Don't forget what I said once before, lovey," she cautioned. "And don't take too much notice of Tim if you don't want to! You're Ann's friend as well as ours, remember, and we love you for yourself, anyway."

"Thanks." Molly felt suddenly awkward, but Joan glossed over the moment and it passed without further incident, even when Molly said she would like to go to church with the old lady on Christmas morning.

"Jolly good idea," Joan said with unexpected enthusiasm. "I'd like to go myself. If you'll trust to my driving, and don't mind my little runabout, I'll drive you in and we'll both go. The oven can be set on the timer, and it'll all work out perfectly."

Strangely enough, from that moment everything seemed to move with an astonishing rapidity towards the festive season. Two days later John took Molly to the Children's Home, and there everyone was already in a whirl of preparation for the Great Day.

Molly was enchanted by the children, whose ages ranged from that of small toddlers, born, it seemed, more or less behind invisible bars but bars which were nonetheless real, to those approaching the age when they would shortly have to be trying their wings in the competitive world outside. She was surprised to find most of them spoke two or even three languages, and all of them could make themselves understood in the language of the country which was taking care of them.

She chatted with some boys who had been learning carpentery and joinery. There were others who had been apprenticed to a sympathetic local garage and who were learning car maintenance and motor engineering, while amongst the girls, while there was a preponderance of them who attended the local College of Further Education for domestic cookery, others were earning while learning in a multiple tailors' factory.

All of them, she was surprised to find, were unbelievably happy, and all of them looking forward tremendously towards the Christmas festival. Even the small ones were laboriously making paper chains and had been out in the grounds of the home collecting evergreens for use as decoration.

Driving back to Bronton, Molly could not restrain herself from commenting upon the fact of this obvious happiness.

"One would never realise most of them had such a tragic background to their lives," she said in wonderment. John smiled, and there was something a little grim about the smile which did not escape Molly's notice.

"I always think it's *because* of their tragic backgrounds that they are so grateful for the happiness and safety they enjoy now," he said slowly. "Human nature's odd, Molly. People never seem to value what they've had showered upon them. It's only when they've had to do without something they appreciate it when they do get it, be it safety, contentment, happiness or even money, although," he grinned suddenly, his boyish self once more, "for most of them I think that is the least of their worries," he added. "They've been so accustomed to having to do without things, when they have them— and, in most cases, have achieved them partly by their own efforts—that the satisfaction outweighs everything else. It's psychological, really."

"You seem to know a lot of psychology," Molly teased. "I wonder you didn't specialise?"

"I may yet do that," John said soberly. "The illnesses of the mind fascinate me, as well as its other aspects. I have the strongest feeling that when we know more about what impels one man to steal and another to give away all his worldly goods, we'll have gone a long way towards the curing of a lot of the ills of our present-day society."

He broke off then, pointing to a holly tree in the hedge where the glowing berries gleamed high against the winter sky.

"If you'd like to," he suggested half shyly, "we'll come out here again in about a week's time and collect some evergreens for the centre and for the house. Miss Spofforth won't want anything we bring in. She has a small holly bush which yields enough for her needs—and to give a little towards the decoration of the church each year, she has an apple tree which fosters a small mistletoe plant, and she has a marvellous bed of Christmas roses. Everyone else's Christmas roses seem to appear in January, but hers are always there just in time for Christmas Day."

"Perhaps her prayers help them," Molly said seriously, and to her relief John accepted this quietly.

"Perhaps," he agreed. "I shouldn't be in the least surprised to learn that they do!"

From then onwards she was caught up in a whirl of preparations for the festive week, both in the centre, in the Cottage and everywhere she went. By the time Tim came for her, in the station waggon after the centre closed following evening surgery on Christmas Eve, she was very tired.

"Be sure to rest as much as you can, Molly," John said as she left him. "Dr. Brent is taking first call, Dr. Marsh, from the Tor practice is taking second. Then Dr. Saul, Brent's partner, then Dr. Doyle and lastly myself. Everyone seems to think you and I get the thick end of the stick, metaphorically speaking, being here all the time. They've gone to all this elaborate rigmarole so that we might manage a little complete break ourselves."

"*You* need it, anyway!" was Molly's comment, but looking at the faint purple shadows under her lovely eyes and noting how pale she had become these last few days, John rather felt she was the one who ought to be remember she was still supposed to be on light duties only.

They parted with mutual seasonal good wishes and Molly walked back to Rosewood Cottage, where she had barely time to give Miss Spofforth the lightweight duffle coat and hood which she had bought as a Christmas gift to protect the old lady when she was, as she persisted in doing, working in her garden despite the flurries of snow and the wind, which at times was piercingly cold.

"I'm not really working," Miss Spofforth had protested when Molly had remonstrated with her during the week. "I can't dig, the ground's too hard, and I can't do very much at all, but I like to be out there, and I like to walk about and plan what I'm going to do when spring comes. That's something I always do, Molly. Plan for spring—and summer—the moment the first autumnal chills sound a warning! It's good for the soul."

Certainly it appeared to be equally good for the body, Molly had reflected, noting the rosy cheeks, the sparkling eyes and the erect figure of the woman she had grown to love as much as she had ever loved anyone outside her own family circle before.

She accepted the little fur-trimmed bonnet made by Miss Spofforth's own clever fingers to match the fur gloves she had bought, gave Cat the new dish and bowl she had bought for him and which he inspected carefully and finally appeared to accept, then, as Tim was waiting, they soon were on their way to Beckside.

The roads were icy, and in one way Molly was thankful. Tim's attention was taken up by driving, and there was no opportunity for personal conversation.

At the farm everything was beautifully decorated, and, as always, Molly wondered how Joan found the time to attend to such matters as well as doing her job, the cooking and helping Tim with his bookwork as Molly knew she did some of the evenings she was at home.

She was lovingly embraced and despatched up to the room she had shared with Ann before the accident when her own small bed had been taken down to the office. Here, as everywhere in the big old house, radiators fed by water heated from the huge Aga in the kitchen warmed the atmosphere. Miss Spofforth believed in warmth, and so far Molly had not even been chilled in the house which was her temporary home. Yet the small low fire which fed Miss Spofforth's radiators was as nothing compared with the many radiators all over Beckside, so that the whole house was warmed through, and seemed to bask in its near-summer heat.

Despite the tension of Tim's hovering presence—for everywhere Molly went he followed—and the fact that he was obviously trying to manipulate the opportunity for a private talk, they were all kept briskly busy by a bustling Joan.

On Christmas Eve they sat and watched the television, and Molly thought of Ann and the others walking round the wards, singing the well-loved carols, and her eyes were a little misty. When her parents were abroad as now, Christmas at Tunby had come to mean a great deal to the girl, but she was determined to find the same happiness here, with her friends.

Christmas Day was especially festive. True to her promise, Joan brought out the small car she used herself and she and Joan, well muffled against the cold, drove to church. They saw John and Miss Spofforth, who chatted a moment, then bustled away to be sure everything would be in readiness for her visitor when he arrived.

"It's a busy day for the Vicar!" she explained as she parted from them both with mutual good wishes. "Happy Christmas!"

They arrived back at Beckside glowing and happy, and, as Joan remarked, "Having been to church it seems I'm set right for all the rest of Christmas," which appeared to effectively sum up the situation.

People arrived and departed all the afternoon, and Molly lost count of the number of friends and neighbours, some of whom she recognised as patients, others she had never seen before, to whom she was introduced as Ann's friend, from Tunby.

During the afternoon the telephone rang with John at the other end asking anxiously if she would consent to accompany him to the party at the Children's Home the afternoon of Boxing Day.

"I know it's Ann's one day at home," he apologised. "Of course she might like to come too, and she'd be very welcome . . . but Matron asked especially if you would be there."

"I'd love to go," Molly said sincerely. "I don't know about Ann, of course. She may want to stay with the family . . . but I can ask her when she comes. Tim's meeting her from the coach in the early hours of the morning."

"She'll be tired," John prophesied. "She may want to rest until evening. When will she be due back?"

"Morning of the day after Boxing Day," Molly began, then hastily corrected herself. "Sorry," she said. "She's on change-over. She's to be back for night duty; I remember Joan saying so now."

"Then she'll be catching the midday coach the day after Boxing Day," John announced. "She'll get into Tunby around five, then. Just time for a brief rest and refresher before duty begins. Sounds exhausting, even to think of it!"

They chatted a few minutes longer, then she turned from the phone to find Tim beside her.

"You're not planning on leaving us until after Boxing Day, are you?" he asked abruptly.

"Not until time for morning surgery on that day," Molly smiled, but he continued to look forbidding. "Your mother's promised I can go in with her when she goes to surgery, so there's no hurry. Why?" she added gently, as his expression didn't lighten.

"Because I want a private word with you before you do leave, Molly. That's why," Tim said. Before she could make any comment he had turned and gone into one of the rooms leading off from the hall which, as she well knew, was crowded with visitors. Quietly and feeling strangely and inexplicably saddened, she turned and followed him.

CHAPTER FIVE

BY the time Sophie, the girl who helped around Beckside Farm, had brought tea and toast to Molly as she called her the following morning, Ann was snugly in the twin bed at the other side of the boarded-up fireplace.

Molly sipped her tea and looked at her friend. She must have come into the bedroom as quietly as a mouse, Molly reflected, and Tim must have been just as quiet when he had driven off to collect his sister from the coach station.

Ann looked tired, but she had the peaceful sleep of one who was resting after work well and truly done, and with satisfaction. Equally quietly herself, Molly dressed and went downstairs to find Joan and Sophie already busy in the kitchen.

" 'Morning, lovey," Joan answered her greeting, saying at the same time she was to rest, everything was done. There was to be cold turkey for Boxing Day, with a special Christmas pudding, as Sophie called it, especially in honour of the returned daughter of the family. By lunch-time Ann had awakened; Molly remembered only too well how easy it was, when once it had become a habit, to awaken at whatever hour one informed one's subconscious mind one wished to be astir.

They spent what was left of the early part of the day talking about Tunby General and about the people they both knew who worked there. Only one name was omitted from the discussion, as though by mutual consent. Ann did not mention Flint Cardew, and although she wondered how he was progressing—and his affair with the wonderful Fiona—Molly could not bring herself to ask the question.

She was a little disappointed, but not surprised, when Ann said she would rather spend the afternoon talking to her mother, catching up on family news, than attend the Children's Home party.

"I helped at two in the Children's Ward," she excused herself, "and with the ward party, and I feel I've had enough for this year. There'll be the New Year celebrations when I get back. I know those aren't quite so hectic as a rule, but when you're on night duty they're tiring enough, especially with Matron's dance in the same week!"

Molly could understand and well sympathise, and if she had been less than honest with herself she would never have admitted to the little thrill she knew she was feeling as she and Dr. Maitland drove off together to the Home.

The children, youngsters and teenagers alike, seemed delighted to see them. They proudly showed them both the wonderful decorations they had made themselves, and the equally wonderful gifts, mostly miracles of ingenuity, which they had made for each other and for the few members of the staff.

Both Molly and John were delighted by the afternoon, and when at last, after a lovely tea of special dishes made by the girls from the cookery classes, they left for home, Molly heaved a sigh of mingled contentment and envy.

"Why the sigh?" John asked, noting her expression. "They've had a wonderful time. I don't think they want you to feel sorry for them just now."

"I don't," Molly said candidly. "In fact, in a way I envy them. They seem so contented by so little in a material sense, and yet they have so much—now—in the love for one another, the joy of sharing, the . . . it sounds silly, but it's what I feel . . . the curious feeling of unity which seems to embrace them all."

"If that same feeling had embraced the whole of mankind before the world went mad," John said solemnly, "there wouldn't have been any need for places like that. There wouldn't have been such people to fill them, and homes like that can be multiplied all over the country, all over the so-called civilised world."

"No today!" Molly said in a strangely pleading tone, so that he looked at her in some surprise. "Don't let's spoil today with thoughts of things which have spoiled life for so many people," she begged. He caught her mood, stopped at a little wayside hotel and pulled into the courtyard.

"It's not often I do this," he explained, "but somehow I'd like to drink a Christmas toast with you before the season's over. A drink to *next* Christmas, although goodness knows what will have happened by then."

Molly smiled and followed him into the small lounge, where the landlord evidently recognised him at once.

"Compliments of the season, Doctor," he began as he took their order. "Pity you weren't by a little while ago. I believe your folks look after that journalist chappie, don't you? Mr. Germain, he's called, I think."

"That's right." John accepted the drinks and paid, raising his glass to Molly. "What's happened?"

"He came in just around lunch-time," the landlord announced. "As you know, it's almost time to close now, and he'd had more than enough to drink when he arrived here. He was driving himself, of course, and Mrs. Judd advised him not to have anything more. He became . . . abusive, I suppose you'd call it. Then he got really nasty and began smashing glasses and so on. I took a hand there, as you'll imagine, and when he wouldn't see sense I had to call P.C. Burdows. He came along, and *he* called Farrowby. It's as near to Farrowby as it is to the Cottage, and anyway we're really over the boundary."

"What happened?" Molly asked. She had listened in horrified silence throughout, hoping nothing she had said over the phone had been any sort of contributory factor towards this outburst.

"They've taken him in for observation, miss," the landlord said flatly. "Seems they think they can cure him of wanting to drink so much. Might be a blessing if they can. Mrs. Judd says he was a good journalist before he started that caper."

"It'll do him all the good in the world," John said quietly. "Mr. Barnes, head of the psychiatric clinic at Farrowby, is a clever man. He's in the right hands. I'm sure it will all work out well for him in the long run."

Molly wished she could have felt just as certain, but she could not, any more than she could feel anything but relief when hour after hour went by and, try as he might, Tim found no opportunity to see her alone, not even for a moment.

The relief ended when Ann went upstairs to pack her overnight case, Joan disappeared into the kitchen to pack a box of goodies to make snacks of when she was too tired to keep awake, as she put it. Sophie was upstairs making the beds, and there was no one else around as Tim followed Molly into the lounge and came to sit beside her before the fire.

"I'm not accusing you of avoiding me, Molly," he said with heavy seriousness, "but it does seem like trying to catch a hold of the will-o'-the-wisp to try and have a private word with you!"

"I'm here now, anyway," Molly said, obviously. "What is it?"

"I don't like you getting so involved with all these extra things, Molly," Tim began heavily. "There's the surgery. I can understand that, because a person like yourself—like Mum—needs to follow her own work or she'll be miserable! Then there's this home—I ought to say *these* homes—they're not for the likes of you to work in or for! Social workers are what are wanted there, and the folks' own initiative. You give out enough of yourself, working in the surgery all day. Or is it," he asked with sudden penetration, "because you don't see enough of Dr. Maitland, being with him most of the day and living practically next door to him as well? Isn't that it?" he persisted. "Haven't you been hurt enough by the one doctor who was supposed to think the world of you?"

Molly sprang to her feet. No one, not even Tim, could put John in the same category as Flint Cardew. When she had first known Flint she had, she realised, put him on a pedestal, idolised him, and that had been a very mistaken thing to do. Now John, although until this moment he had not realised it, had taken his place in her mental image of the ideal man. In him she could see Chaucer's version of the 'parfait gentil knight', and she hated to hear him referred to in this fashion, even though she knew Tim didn't really mean what he was saying—or she hoped he didn't.

"Dr. Maitland's a very different kind of person, Tim," she said with a quietness which, if he had known her better, would have told him she was really very angry. "He's not in the least like the social-climbing, money-conscious person who is Dr. Cardew! They're two very different people."

"But you're the same girl!" Tim flashed. "And they both want you—or rather both thought they did—do—I mean Dr. Cardew did and now Dr. Maitland does," he managed, gradually losing some of his anger in the small confusion in which he found himself.

"You're being particularly foolish, Tim," Molly managed as quietly as she could. "Dr. Cardew and I . . . ." she stopped, recovered herself and carried on in an even tone, "we made a mistake," she said firmly, definitely, "and we realised that in time. Dr. Maitland and I work together, just that and nothing more. Can't you understand I don't want any emotional involvement for a long time to come? I want to be myself for a time."

"You can be yourself with me, Molly," Tim burst out impetuously. "I'd never prevent you doing anything you wanted to do, you know that, don't you? I'd look after you, shield you from . . . everything . . ."

"But it's no use, Tim," Molly interrupted as gently as she could, hushing him as he would have spoken again. "I don't love you, you see," she almost whispered. "I don't love anyone . . . not in that way. I *thought* I loved Flint Cardew—no, I'm not sure I ever thought of it as *loving* him—I was enamoured by him, I thought him wonderful, but so far above me it was a miracle when he even spoke, let alone when he first asked me to go out with him!"

"Don't!" Tim said sharply. "Don't talk like that, Molly! It was wonderful for him—it must have been—to have *you* go out with *him*, and how he could hurt you as he did. . . . And it doesn't matter about not loving me either," he rushed on before she could speak. "I've enough love for the two of us, and I'll teach you to share it."

"Thank you, but no," Molly said, so firmly that he

was silenced abruptly. "I don't want love, not yet," she went on decidedly. "I want to be of service to as many people as I can. I want to give and give of all the things I've been taught, and all the things I've learned—especially these past months—without being taught. I don't think I'm even ready for that sort of love just yet," she went on candidly. "I want to work at the Homes, to work at the centre, and, when I'm well enough, go back to Tunby General and get my Sister's cap. I don't know what I want after that," she admitted. "But I do know I'll find out, if I go on the path I chose when I became a nurse. That's all I'm sure of right now."

"And Dr. Maitland?" Tim persisted. "What does he say about all this?"

"We haven't discussed it," Molly said coldly. "You don't seem to understand. We *work* together, that's all."

"He's a man, isn't he?" Tim demanded crudely, Molly thought with an inward shudder. "If you won't say you'll marry me . . . not just yet, anyway, at least let me buy an engagement ring—anything you like—and he'll know there's someone to look out for you, watch your interests in the future. He won't be able to turn on you when you need him, if ever you do, like the other one did!"

"Don't talk any more like that!" Molly's patience was exhausted and she was suddenly frightened of the blazing light in Tim's eyes, of the eager manner in which he moved towards her. "I shall be back on duty at the centre tomorrow," she said crisply. "Don't let's spoil what's left of this holiday, please!"

"There are twelve days of Christmas," Tim said, unabashed. "What do you plan to do with the rest of them?"

"That carol's a relic of old England," Molly said

tartly. "I don't suppose I shall do anything with the rest of the festive season, except go to the Watch Night service with Miss Spofforth. I did promise to do that. Why?"

"No reason," Tim moved away. "I just thought maybe we could talk about this again some time," he said quietly. "That's all."

"We'll see," Molly said in evasive relief. "I'm not in the least sure that I want to talk about it, but I'm sure I shan't change my mind!"

"I can hope, anyhow," Tim said firmly. "You can't prevent my doing that!"

The argument appeared to be ended, and at that moment Sophie came in to collect the things to set the tea-table, so that no further conversation was possible, for which Molly was truly thankful.

The remainder of her visit passed without incident. The following morning she bade Ann good-bye and gave her so many messages to other people at Tunby General that Ann laughingly protested she ought to have a notebook to write them all down, and still neither of them mentioned Flint. Only when Molly was putting on her coat ready to leave with Joan did Ann turn to her abruptly and say quietly :

"Let Tim down gently, love, won't you? I'd have loved you as a sister, but I know it wouldn't work out. When you've gone back to Tunby—or found someone else—" she smiled mysteriously, "then he'll remember that Jean Purvey, the girl who manages the dairy farm for Mr. Poole since he had a stroke, is mad about him and always has been. He thought a lot about her until you arrived, and, much as I love you, she and he would make a much more ideal couple for the kind of life Tim leads!"

They laughed together, as they had done ever since they had first become friends. Molly's heart lightened, for she knew with real certainty that whatever happened between herself and Tim, her friendship with Ann wasn't going to be impaired, and she was pleased.

Back at the centre everyone in the three villages appeared to be clamouring for appointments and Liz worked frantically at the switchboard each morning, while the three nurses were finding it more and more difficult to fit in everyone who appeared to be requiring medical attention.

"Most of 'em are genuine enough," Liz observed after elevenses the morning of the last day of the old year, "but some of them are nothing more than the natural results of over-eating, over-drinking and general self-indulgence!"

Joan, washing her hands, laughed heartily at this wholesale condemnation of the majority of humanity by such a young person, but Betty's sad face was lightened just a little by a smile of warm sympathy.

"I know how you feel, Liz," she said solemnly. "There are times when I would love to point out to some of them that they could cure themselves by a little forethought. They wouldn't need a cure, half of them, if they'd think first. You've only to think of Mr. Germain, for instance."

"I wondered what had happened to him," Molly murmured, ashamed to remember she hadn't even given the man another thought after the episode when she and John had learned what had happened to him.

"He's in the Psychiatric Unit, undergoing a cure," Betty said, and her face turned a gentle pink. "I . . . I've gone there on my free day for a long time," she sounded ashamed. "I think it's as little as one can do to help. I *couldn't* nurse there, but I go round with the book trolley and things like that and chat to some of the patients who've no one to visit them. I've spent a lot of time with Alex—with Mr. Germain—since he went there at the beginning of the week. He's not all that's bad, you know!" she said defensively, although no one had even hinted that he was. "He told me that when he was younger he saw what a hell life was made for people who cared too deeply for others, and he made up his mind when he was a young man to care for nobody. He's kept that vow, but it's given him this warped outlook on life, and now, I think, he's seeing the other side of the coin."

"I'm glad, Betty." Joan had dried her hands now and was quietly massaging cream into them from the small tube she carried in her bag. "If anything can heal him, someone to understand will do the trick." She didn't add 'and someone to care for will heal you too, my girl,' but as clearly as if she had spoken the words aloud Molly could sense them winging their soundless way to the heart of the other girl.

"I promised I'd go to the Watch Night service and say a prayer for him," Betty continued, going even pinker and suddenly becoming confused. "I don't know what effect he thinks it will have, but he asked me to do it, and I promised."

"I'll see you there, then," Molly broke the slight tension by the announcement. "I promised I'd go with Miss Spofforth. I was surprised when she said she was going, because she's such a staunch churchgoer, but when I looked surprised she astonished me by reminding me, 'We're all aiming for the same place, aren't we? so what difference does it make which route we follow?' and there wasn't any answer to that either!"

A general discussion as to the relative merits of one place of worship as opposed to another broke out, and had—as always happens—reached no final conclusion when it was time to leave.

"See you later, then," Betty called, and hurried off, and Molly, muffled up to the ears against the shrill wind which had sprung up all at once, was thankful to let herself into Rosewood Cottage and the comfort of Miss Spofforth's shining little home.

Cat and his mistress had, so the old lady said, enjoyed their Christmas. Now they were looking forward to tomorrow, when Miss Spofforth assured Molly that she would be pleasantly surprised by her New Year dinner. Amused and mystified, the girl ate her evening meal, changed her clothes and prepared to brave the buffeting wind for the second time that evening, marvelling at the determination of the elderly lady who, facing the wind, announced that this would blow the cobwebs away.

It would, Molly felt, blow more than cobwebs away! It seemed likely to take them from their feet, but they managed to fight their way along the main street and to the far end where, a village distant from the church, the chapel stood, lights streaming out into the night.

The simplicity of the service, the words of the hymns, the united voices hushed in prayer seemed balm to Molly, who had felt as buffeted by Tim's words mentally as she had felt physically buffeted by the wind. Here in the chapel, as in the church, there was peace and calm, and she felt uplifted as the two of them, after greeting Betty whom they saw in the porch, made their way back to Rosewood Cottage.

Cat seemed delighted by their safe return, and in moments Miss Spofforth had produced the creamy cocoa she seemed always to have on hand these cold nights.

"You won't mind if I take mine up to bed, will you, love?" she asked. "I'm tired, I think. It must have been the wind which was stronger than I'd realised. How you stand up to things like that after a day at the centre, and when you're not supposed to do much as yet, I really don't know!" the old lady marvelled. "You ought to take more care of yourself, you know!"

"Don't scold, not tonight!" Molly begged. "My new year's resolution is to do all I can to get back to my proper work as soon as ever I can ... but I won't like leaving you and Cat!"

"Only Cat and myself?" Miss Spofforth's eyes twinkled as she unexpectedly leaned forward and kissed the girl. "Happy New Year, love," she said a little chokily. "I haven't had anyone in my house at the first hour of any year since I can remember! This is something special, and I like it."

She liked it too, Molly decided, sitting by the stove and sipping her cocoa, Cat purring at her feet and yet ready and waiting to trot upstairs to his basket. She stroked his head absentmindedly, thinking of nothing in particular, but a jumble of the thoughts of Miss Spofforth's lonely life, that of Alex Germain, that of Betty Taylor, and those of the people in the two Homes, alone and yet together.

"It seems funny," she mused, "to know so little—and yet so much—about so many people and yet not to know just what goes on inside their minds, what makes them do things. I'd like to know more about all that. I wonder if Dr. Maitland has any books he would lend me. . . ."

Her thoughts were shattered by a gentle but persistent tapping on the door. Wondering if Betty had decided to call and chat for a while, she went quietly through the scullery and drew the bolt. She almost let out a cry of alarm when Tim's broad-shouldered form filled the doorway.

"Let me come in for a minute, Molly," he pleaded. "I waited until I saw the old lady's light go on in the front bedroom. I've *got* to talk to you!"

"What's the matter?" Molly asked, keeping her voice to a whisper, afraid of trusting the sharp-eared old lady upstairs.

"Let me in, and I'll tell you," Tim said stubbornly. "It's freezing, out here in the wind!"

She couldn't disbelieve him. The walk home from the chapel and chilled her to the bone and, after being so warmly cosy by the stove, standing here at the open door, she already felt very cold herself. Cat, after one investigating sniff, had retreated and was curled up in front of the Aga, but Molly felt he was watchful and distrusting, and abruptly, but distinctly, she shared his instincts.

"Just for a minute, then," she said cautiously. "I don't know what Miss Spofforth would say ... you'd better not make a sound. She always reads for at least an hour, and she'll be angry if she knows I've invited you in at this time of the morning."

"You didn't, if that's any comfort to your conscience!" Tim grinned. "I practically pushed my way in. Short of physical violence I don't think you'd have kept me out!"

"Would you like some cocoa?" Molly asked the question almost automatically, and yet in a way she was conscious she was deliberately prolonging the moment when he would have to say what was the reason for this visit. "The jug's half full," she added, pointing.

"In a minute," Tim ignored the jug of steaming, fragrant liquid. "I came to see you, without anyone else being around. Why are you staying here, Molly? What's the attraction? It can't be Miss Spofforth, although I've nothing against the old dear, so it must be Dr. Maitland. I'd have thought you'd had enough of doctors."

Molly's self-control seemed to snap. She didn't want to discuss Flint Cardew with anyone, not ever, and certainly had she wanted to do so the last person she would have chosen as a confidant would have been Tim.

"I'm staying here because I want to," she said frostily. "It's the nearest thing I can find to the job I'm trained to do, and I like it, and I *love* Miss Spofforth ... and Cat," she concluded as that sagacious animal twitched his ears at the mention of the name of his beloved mistress.

"You could come back to Beckside, marry me, and in all probability get taken on at the Cottage when you're strong enough," Tim said quickly. "I've thought it all out. We could...."

"*You* could go home now!" Molly's glance snapped dangerously. "I want to go back to Tunby when I'm all right, when I nurse again, not stay here, working at the Cottage where I don't know anyone or living with your mother, when she knows my working ambitions are of an entirely different nature." She had a sudden flash of memory, and, feeling mean, she lashed out: "I don't know what went wrong between you and the girl who manages the dairy farm for Mr. Poole," she knew all about Mr. Poole, anyhow. He was one of Dr. Doyle's patients. "I know you were more than friends...."

"That's over and done with," Tim said sullenly, but he was evidently surprised to know she even knew of Jean's existence. 'Ann or Mum,' he thought blankly. 'I ought to have known! They both thought we made an ideal pair.'

Shutting down the memory of the fact that once, not so long ago either, he had thought the same thing he forced from his mind the idea that the attraction of the slim girl who faced him might be nothing more than the attraction of finding someone new, on the rebound, he believed the phrase ran.

"I'd better go," he made towards the door and she didn't try to keep him, not for a second. "Anyhow, you know what I've been thinking, if you change your mind when you've had time to think it over and see it'd work."

"I don't need time to think it over, thank you," Molly said decisively, following him to the door and closing it as his tall form retreated down the path. "Good-night!" she called belatedly. "I shall do my best to forget all about this visit, and I'd advise you to do the same! No one need ever know you've called, and I certainly shan't broadcast the fact."

He knew she was meaning that no word of his visit would reach the ears of Jean Purvey, not even from a chance remark of hers, but he angrily raced his engine and switched on his headlights before scorching off down the road which led him back to Beckside.

A few doors further along the road John started as he heard the sound of the racing engine. Walking to his gate, he saw the light streaming from the open door, then it closed and the light was gone, but, he noticed almost automatically, the light still shone from the upstairs window which he knew full well belonged to Miss Spofforth's bedroom.

Was that the Beckside car he had just seen travelling at speed down the road? It couldn't have been because anyone at the farm was ill, since Joan would have phoned him, and Mrs. Burton would have left a message because she knew he was out. It was his night on call, and there had been an accident at the Five Lane Ends crossroads. He had just returned from the Cottage where two of the people involved in the crash had been taken.

"Then why?" he asked himself aloud as he bolted the garage door and went through the connecting one into his home, "why was Molly standing at the door, obviously seeing her mysterious visitor off the premises, and yet, if whoever it was had accompanied herself and Miss Spofforth to the Watch Night service, the spinster lady would not have gone to bed with her book. She was too fond of conversation, as opposed to simply talk, to have missed one moment of a visitor's company.

"It was someone for Molly," John reasoned, "and I'd stake my life that was Tim Flecker's car! There isn't another one in Bronton has an engine which sounds like that!" It was one of his peculiarities upon which he prided himself. Before the group centre had opened he had always known which of his many patients who had cars had just arrived. He was, he supposed, particularly sensitive to the different sounds of the varying engines!

"If that's how the land lies," he mused as he absent-mindedly walked into his own trim kitchen and picked up the tray and thermos flask Mrs. Burton always left for him when he was on call, "then it's time I stopped dreaming dreams."

He went quietly to bed, but not to sleep for what seemed like hours. After Elaine he had resolved never to allow another woman to mean anything to him more than a friend, and a friend with reservations at that!

But Molly wasn't like any other woman! She wasn't beautiful, as Elaine had been. She was ... he sought for the words ... attractive, and with an attractive and stimulating personality. Yet it was more than that!

The glossy dark-gold hair, the wide-open blue eyes

fringed as they were with those thick dark lashes which had made Betty say they looked as though they'd been put in with a smutty finger, and the generous red mouth were pleasing enough. It was the way in which her sympathies flowed out to those in distress, the manner in which she identified herself with those in pain, whether of mind or body. It was the uncanny manner she had of expressing just what he was feeling or thinking and somehow hadn't found the right words with which to express himself. It was all of that and more.

John thumped his pillow in exasperation. He hadn't even said one word to her which might not have been overheard by the entire population of the three villages. He'd taken her to the two homes for which he worked so hard and with such an intense interest, and he had felt she shared his feelings and emotions there.

He didn't know why she bothered him, or even in what way. He wasn't imagining himself in love with her or anything like that, he told himself furiously. He simply wanted to be certain she was ... what was the word he was seeking? ... emotionally all right. That was it, he informed the dimmed light beside his bed. She'd taken a terrific toss from that horse of young Flecker's. She'd been lucky not to be killed. At the same time she'd taken a terrific emotional toss from the man to whom she was engaged, and she'd survived both, apparently quite well.

"Then if she's interested in young Flecker what's that to do with *you*?" he demanded of himself, but he knew perfectly well that if Molly had been interested in Tim Flecker, then she would have let him know, one way or another, on the runs they had shared together to the two homes, or when they had met in the course of any working day.

"I feel Joan would have dropped a hint, too," he told himself. Yet, if she wasn't interested in young Tim, then why had he been visiting her, after midnight, when all—or most—of the inhabitants of the three villages were safely in bed, even those who had been out to the Watch Night service?

It was more than he could understand, and at long last, after more turning and tossing than he could remember ever having gone through in one night, not even when he had parted company with Elaine, he fell into an exhausted sleep from which Mrs. Burton finally had to arouse him by the making of fresh hot, strong coffee which he favoured in the mornings.

He was on time at the surgery, although it had meant leaving a good half of the substantial breakfast he normally enjoyed. He picked up his list of appointments, glancing keenly at Molly as he did so, but to his surprise she looked alarmingly the same as she always looked, and not even tired.

Unreasonably annoyed, he spoke curtly, requesting that two of the names of the list should be transposed and their owners so informed before afternoon appointments.

"They're both on the phone," he said crossly. "Make what excuse you consider suitable."

Molly looked at John in bewilderment. Normally Dr. Maitland was the most even-tempered of all five members of the centre.

"Something must have upset him," Joan offered, adding : "It may be something to do with that accident at Five Lane Ends last night. He was on call, wasn't he?"

Molly nodded and agreed that there might well be some connection, but privately she didn't think so. John was not the sort of doctor to allow extra work to interfere with either his efficiency or his temper. Whatever it was, she decided, it must be something more personal than being kept at the Cottage a good part of the night because of someone's emergency.

Whatever it was, she found his manner more and more curt as the morning wore on. She wasn't to know that every time he caught a glimpse of her as she showed one or another of his patients in to him, he found himself wondering whether or not young Flecker had kissed her good-night last night, and if he had, had she found the experience enjoyable ... and was it the first time?

Knowing nothing of the thoughts which were tormenting him, and aware only that his ill-humour appeared to be directly and solely sent in her direction, Molly at first felt sorry for him, then angry, and, lastly, upset.

"I can't think what I've done!" she practically wailed to Joan. "Has he often been like this?"

"I've only known him behave this way twice in all the time I've known him," Joan admitted, "and that's when he first joined his late father in the practice here. Something—or someone—must have upset him. Maybe it was being at that accident most of the night. I know he'd been to a difficult birth earlier. I saw Nurse Jarvis," she mentioned the local midwife, "as I came this morning, and she said what a time they'd had with Mrs. Armstrong and her first. A breech, it was," she added as an extra item of passing interest.

"He wasn't like that when he looked in at the Psychiatric Unit, anyway," Betty spoke up suddenly, blushing as she had suddenly started to do these days. "I popped up there before I came to work this morning," she went on almost apologetically. "I wanted to wish Alex a happy new year. His mother was a Scotswoman, you see, and he thinks a great deal of Hogmanay, as he calls it."

"And you saw Dr. Maitland?" Joan asked before Betty could lapse into one of her now frequent long discussions about Alex Germain.

"Oh, no!" Betty looked shocked. "I just left Alex a wee gift for the new year, and he said the doctor had looked in on him before he left, just after midnight, and that he thought it was mighty nice of him, when he was so busy here."

Molly said nothing more. She listened, and gradually it dawned upon her that whatever had occasioned the strange complexity of John's present mood, had happened some time after the Watch Night service had ended and, presumably, after the accident had been dealt with.

"It can't be something I've done, at that rate," she told herself firmly. "He knew I was going to the service with Miss Spofforth, and I didn't see him any more after evening surgery until I arrived here this morning and found him like a bear with a sore head!" She tried, but in no way could throw off the feeling that in some way his strange mood was something to do with herself and her doings. He wasn't, she noticed, half so short and curt with the others as he was with her. It was true that his patients and his appointments were *her* responsibility, and had little or nothing to do with either Joan or Betty, and even less to do with Nurse Banstead, who almost always was at the centre when John and Molly were not, but when either of the two partners to whose practice she had been attached was on duty.

Even when the morning appointments were completed and the last patient had departed, John's manner did not change. She had no idea as to how sternly he was holding himself in check, half-afraid he might yet burst out with a question as to who the man was he had seen leaving Rosewood Cottage the previous early morning. To prevent himself from saying any such thing he deliberately kept his manner curt and his words almost to monosyllables, so that by the time she went off duty Molly was thoroughly miserable, convinced she had failed in some way which, as yet, she did not understand.

It did not take Miss Spofforth long to decide something was very wrong indeed where her boarder was concerned. Even when Cat came to greet her, rubbing round her legs and purring, the old lady noticed Molly was abstracted and withdrawn, seemingly lost in her own thoughts. Wise in her generation, Miss Spofforth made no comment. She went on talking about the new bowl of African violets which someone had brought her that morning to welcome the year, and about how her specially prepared bulbs were now bursting into flower, at long last.

"They seem to know they were planned to come forth for Christmas and are determined to make a specially brave show now to make up for being a week late," she announced as she dished up the savoury omelette she had made for lunch. "I think that's the nicest thing about a bulb," she chattered on companionably, completely ignoring the fact that Molly was evidently only half listening.

"You buy an oval or round brown object, hard and uninteresting-looking, something in the nature of a screwed-up bit of brown paper with a stone in the middle, and a wizened old onion, losing its skin, and end up with a miracle of beauty! That's one of the reasons I'd never be an atheist," she declared, à propos of nothing.

"I . . . I'm sorry," Molly said apologetically. "I didn't hear what you were saying. I'm afraid my thoughts were miles away."

"I was saying," Miss Spofforth didn't mind repeating what she considered was quite an original remark, "one of the reasons why I'd never be an atheist is because such unexpected beauty lies hidden under the most unconvincing exterior, like a lovely flower of a hyacinth emerging from something which looked, when you put it into the fibre, rather like a wizened old onion, and that," she ended dramatically, "not even fit for the stewpot."

In spite of her unaccountably heavy heart, Molly smiled. Her landlady was a most extraordinary woman, she thought, not for the first time. She made an effort to rally her thoughts and to reply in kind.

"I know what you mean," she said softly. "Like the people whom you'd never expect to ever be curt and short-tempered without good reason and who suddenly behave that way."

"Dr. Maitland?" Miss Spofforth had only hazarded a guess, but she felt certain Molly never now thought of that young 'fancy doctor', as the old lady thought of Flint, to whom she'd been engaged when she had first come to Bronton.

"Yes," Molly said fervently. "Like Dr. Maitland. I don't know what's upset him this morning, but he's been like a bear with a sore head ever since we opened surgery. But only where I've been concerned! Everyone else has been all right . . . I've apparently done and said everything wrong, although," she ended with a little self-conscious glow of virtue, "even he couldn't find any fault with my work, not really. He seems to have just been grumbling for the sake of hearing his own voice. Not a bit like himself." She hesitated a moment, then added: "Perhaps he's overworking," hopefully waiting for her landlady's reply.

"Perhaps." Miss Spofforth was non-committal. She went on serving the stewed fruit and cream and the slices of wafer-thin bread and butter which she had produced in lieu of a pudding. "He ought to have a partner!"

"There isn't anyone, without advertising," Molly was repeating what John had said so often that Miss Spofforth knew instinctively whose words she was using. "John...Dr. Maitland," she corrected herself quickly, "says he can't imagine anyone else sharing that consulting room now his father's gone."

"They never did like change very much, neither he nor his father, my dear," Miss Spofforth said. Unseen by the girl her eyes took on a lovingly sympathetic look. There was, she felt, more in this little spot of trouble than met the eye, and she wondered vaguely if John's mood had anything to do with the mysterious visitor of the previous night-cum-morning, whose arrival, and departure, she had heard as she lay with her book propped open but unread beside her.

"Nothing *has* changed," Molly protested, "only Dr. Maitland himself. He's not the same person today...."

Her voice trailed into silence, and Miss Spofforth's heart contracted as she suddenly saw what was wrong.

"The child's in love with him and doesn't know it," she decided. "I wonder if he's realised it or whether he's fallen in love with her and hasn't the good sense to say so! It's time someone took a hand here, I think, before they make a mulloch of things altogether!" When she was upset—which was rarely, since that was something she would not permit herself to be—she often mentally relapsed into the country words of her old nanny, words remembered from childhood, not always clear in their meaning, but with an uncanny power to express what they felt.

"Bulbs and folks are much alike, after all," she said, and Molly gave her a startled glance, knowing full well that, if she could find it, there would be some sound reason for that seemingly foolish remark. She waited.

"Everybody's got a soul, a mind and a load of emotions," Miss Spofforth observed. "The trouble is we don't see them at all—or we almost always don't—until they're clothed in a body, and a body's like the wrapping round the bulb, it often protects—or hides, if you like—the beauty and love beneath." She shot a curious glance at the girl, but Molly did not speak. "Dr. Maitland," she went on, "spends his emotions, most of his love and care on those folks at the two homes, and on all the people who come to him as patients. I often wonder if he's anything left over for himself out of it all!"

"If there's something worrying him or upsetting him," Molly said with grim determination, "I'd have thought we'd become good enough friends for him to say so, without going off like a spoiled child. He's behaving like ... like Flint, when he wanted all his own way!" she said aggrievedly. "And if he hasn't changed his mood by this afternoon, then I just don't want to know! He's not the same person today as he's been all the time I've known him ... and I don't much like the change!"

CHAPTER SIX

IT was not often Miss Spofforth allowed anything to upset her. Over the years, despite many adverse happenings which, in some curious way, often turned out to be a blessing in disguise, she had evolved a philosophy of her own.

"Given time," she would tell herself firmly, "all things, no matter how trying at the time, usually work out for good in the long run. It's a matter of holding on, and believing everything is going to work out right!"

She relied so firmly on this instinct which she would have been astonished to hear the Vicar describe as he had often done to his friends, 'the truly remarkable faith of my parishioner, Miss Sarah Spofforth.' To her there was nothing remarkable about it. She always took her problems of each and every day, to One she was certain would never fail to help, and so far He had not failed.

When Molly had gone off to the first of the afternoon appointments Miss Spofforth retired to her bedroom, Cat accustomed to these afternoon and evening sessions, accompanying her to settle himself on the window seat and wait.

There *was* a problem, Miss Spofforth was well aware of that, but what was its nature, and how the solving of the difficulty was to be accomplished, she hadn't the faintest idea. That was the least of her worries. She knelt and concentrated; she concentrated so intensely that her head began to ache and Cat moved restlessly on the wide window seat, mewing imperatively.

At the sound Miss Spofforth rose stiffly from her knees and took him into her arms, huddling his soft warmth closely to her. Cat didn't approve, but because she was the one person whom he had loved from kittenhood upwards, he suffered her embrace for a long moment.

"I'll get you some more milk," she told him. "It'll be all right now, Cat. I don't know how or when or why, but it *will* be all right, and before long too, I *know*!"

Cat swished his tail in appreciation of the bowl of creamy milk which his mistress set before him. Watching his small pink tongue flick in and out, imbibing the creamy drops, Miss Spofforth sighed. How much more simple life would be if only the needs of humans could be as easily satisfied as those of her beloved pet!

"I wonder how Molly's getting along?" she pondered aloud, and then gave herself a little mental shake. That was no sign she had given her problem into other hands in complete trust! This was the mood of the doubting Thomas, as Sarah Spofforth never doubted, once she had spilled out her problems, whatever they might be.

Had she been possessed of any degree of second sight she might not have felt quite so contented. Molly had taken in to Dr. Maitland his first appointment of the evening, when the door of the centre opened with a rush, and a young man flung himself before the reception counter.

He was an attractive young man, Molly decided abstractedly. He was of normal height, but he had a mop of wavy brown hair and the one visible eye was a delightful hazel, and with long lashes which, as he partially closed his eye, made a fan on his cheek.

"I'd like . . . I want to see Dr. Brent, please," he began, and gesticulating with his free hand he pointed to the one clasping an impeccably white handkerchief to his left eye.

Molly was a little nonplussed and tried to explain the routine of the centre and that Dr. Brent would not be on duty there until the following afternoon.

"I shall see him before then," the young man said with a lop-sided grin. "I'm on my way there now, but I'd heard from him that he'd moved his surgery here. . . ."

"What appears to be the trouble, Nurse Watson?" Noiselessly John had opened the door of his consulting room to emit Mr. Appleton, and come straight across the corridor and into the reception hall, frowning.

"I was looking for my cousin, sir," the young man's mode of addressing him made John's eyebrows shoot up until they almost disappeared. Did he, he was wondering, look so much senior to the youngster before him? He couldn't be all those years younger than John himself, but the stranger's next words gave the clue.

"I was going to stay with Aunt Muriel and Uncle George," the young man went on. "They're Dr. Brent's parents, you know. Then, just before I left the port, I was handed this telegram." He held out the crumpled form to John, who received it dubiously. "It says," continued the stranger, "Cousin Eric and his wife will be glad to put me up until Aunt Muriel and Uncle George come home. They went away for Christmas. Silly idea, if you ask me," he continued aggrievedly. "I was on my way to Bronton-by-Water when whatever these chippings are on the road flew up and one of them caught my eye. I thought Eric would be able. . . ."

"You've injured your eye?" John interrupted with practicality. "Come inside and let me look. Nurse. . . ."

Inside the consulting room it did not take very long for John to establish that a small chipping of flint from the newly spread road had evidently flown up from under the wheel of a car and was now superficially placed on the cornea. Under John's direction Molly cocainised the eye, and in a matter of minutes John had applied a pad and the offending flint was safely removed.

"You'll have to come in each morning for a day or two," John told him, "until we're certain there's no danger of an ulcer resulting from your unfortunate mishap. But how," he looked puzzled, "did a chip from the road get into your car, I'd like to know?"

"Open top," the young man said breezily. "I'm in the Merchant Navy, and I don't like being cooped up, not even in a car. Always have the hood down, but I guess Eric was right when he said I ought to wear some form of eye protection! Seems a silly idea really, until something like this happens. Oughtn't I to have gone to hospital?" he continued. "I would have done, but this happened only just down the road, and so far as my memory serves me, it would have been at least another four miles to the Cottage, and twice as far to Farrowby, or have I not remembered correctly?"

"Perfectly correctly, Mr. . . . . ?" John hesitated, and the other quickly supplied his name, producing a service medical card from his wallet.

"I'm Ian Brent," he said briefly. "I wanted to look up as many people as I remembered in the village, but not this way," he grinned.

"You've been here before, then?" Molly was showing him out.

"Once when I was at school," Ian said blithely. "I've often wanted to come back and look round—I had a wonderful holiday here that year, but one thing and another has kept me away." He paused at the door. "You're not from these parts, are you, Nurse?" he asked, his bright eye (the other covered by a sterile pad) gleamed mischievously in her direction.

"No," Molly smiled, and lingered as John's buzzer sounded imperatively, indicating that he was awaiting his next appointment. "I . . . haven't been here very long," she concluded. "And I'm not sure I'll be staying much longer, either."

What had made her say that she never knew. She was suddenly irritated by the assertive sound of the buzzer, repeated as the next patient had not yet been shown into the consulting room. Ian Brent smiled and held out his hand.

"Then we must make the most of the time we're both here, Nurse!" he said cheekily. "You're not engaged or . . . anything, are you?" he concluded with a quick glance from his one good eye at her ringless left hand.

From the consulting room the buzzer sounded again, and Molly, feeling instinctively that she could recognise the sounds of something like the irritation of the morning in its very summons, smiled and almost pushed Ian from the door.

"No," she said briefly. "Not . . . engaged, or anything. Come in tomorrow as the doctor said and we'll think about it before then."

He saluted smartly and leapt down the steps, but she had not time to watch his departure. All the same, despite the imperious summons of the buzzer and the fact that John's greeting to his next patient sounded to her ears a little like his manner of the morning, a faint smile played about her lips as she went back to her appointments sheet.

She couldn't understand herself and wondered whatever had possessed her to react in such a manner.

Normally, at Tunby, if a patient had shown signs of trying to get what Sister Murdoch called 'a wee trifle too friendly, like', he would have been promptly, politely and firmly put in his place. Now, she was well aware, she had all but promised to go out with this astonishing young man who had dropped in on the surgery so unexpectedly. It must have been reaction from John's manner of the morning, she told herself, and found herself hoping he would suggest, as he had done so often, that they went out to one or the other of the Homes that evening.

Surgery was ended. Molly lingered as long as she dared, and there was nothing left to keep her occupied, but still John didn't emerge from the consulting room. The door remained firmly closed, and there was nothing she could do about it. She was not to know he was sitting at his desk, pipe firmly clamped between his teeth, a habit he had when thinking hard, and wondering just what had happened to change Molly from the girl he had believed he was getting to know so well to the one who received visitors—male visitors—after midnight, and then carried on a mild flirtation with a complete stranger right under her employer's nose!

He sat there motionless until the tip-tapping of her small, smartly shod feet went down the path and she was on her way back to Miss Spofforth's. He knew the sound of her footfall. It could never be mistaken with Joan's measured tread, Betty's nervous one or Olive Banstead's, with the 'Sister's glide', as Betty always called her walk, which she had never lost and never would lose to her dying day.

"I'd never have thought it of her!" John tapped out the cold pipe and rose, feeling suddenly forlorn. "I'd never have believed her a flirt . . . I'd have thought. . . ."

but he didn't even finish thinking the thought in his mind. Somehow it was all too painful.

Ian was at the surgery the following morning, and Molly made out an appointment card for him as John had said shortly that he ought to come in two or three mornings until they were sure.

She had no conversation with him, as the surgery was busy, but as she was about to leave for her lunch the telephone rang and to her surprise the grave voice of Dr. Eric Brent addressed her.

"I'm on call tonight, as you probably know, Nurse," he said quietly. "I know this is most unethical, but I understand my young cousin has been into the surgery for treatment and that he is to attend daily for a few days. Is that correct?"

"Quite correct, Doctor," Molly told him. She liked Dr. Brent. He was always so correct, so formal and so courteous, it was next to impossible to imagine him being even distantly related to the young sailor!

"This is strictly off the record," he said now, speaking so quietly that she had to strain to hear. "Ian's not a bad chap, you know, but he has rather a reputation, if you know what I mean? I don't want you to be upset again, Nurse, and I understand he is hoping to take you out before he leaves. I simply wanted to warn you not to take him seriously, and to do so without anyone else being able to overhear. I'm not being ... disloyal," he said awkwardly, and she could imagine his kind, sensitive face flushing with embarrassment, so that she hastened to relieve him of the burden he had placed on himself for her sake.

"I understand, Doctor," she said primly. "Thank you for telling me. I appreciate your thoughtfulness," then she hung up, aware that her own cheeks were flushed and that something she had not suspected lay hidden within her heart had thrilled to realise the stranger had thought her sufficiently attractive to have discussed something of his hopes and intentions, whatever they may be, with his host.

John was still behaving in a strained manner, and she did not know why. He had not asked her to go with him to the Home, although she knew he had been there himself the previous evening, and she had felt strangely shut out. She did not know either that several of the children had asked where she was, and that John had felt as awkward and as embarrassed as she would have done herself in reversed circumstances, for he could give no reason for her absence other than to say she was busy.

If he had taken her with him to the Home, as usual, what happened next might never have happened, but at the back of his mind was a constantly recurring picture of the lighted doorway of Rosewood Cottage and the sound of Tim's car departing up the village street. He could not bring himself to ask her about either sight or sound, and Molly was quite unaware he had seen and heard anything. And so, without either of them really being aware how it came about, as January merged into chill, dank February, it became the custom to see the low rakish sports car outside the gate of Rosewood Cottage, and Miss Spofforth and Cat looking gloomily on from behind the shelter of the lace curtains.

Miss Spofforth did not approve, neither, she felt, did Cat, but there wasn't anything they could do about it except pray—on the lady's part—that Ian's leave would not last much longer. It had appeared to have gone on far too long as it was, and although Miss Spofforth apparently accepted the explanation that Ian's ship was being refitted, it was evident she felt the powers-that-be were taking far too long about doing their job, or else they ought to have found him another berth!

February was ending when Ian announced that he would be leaving Bronton the following week.

"Just time to be a couple of mad March hares, Molly my sweet!" he said. "A whirl round Farrowby, I think. It isn't exactly the high life, but it'll have to do this trip, I'm afraid. I'm running just a little too short of cash to go up town and go wild properly."

Molly did not mind in the least. To tell the truth she was growing more than a little tired of Ian's type of conversation, of Ian's ideas of amusement, which always appeared to consist of exactly the same sort of thing, over and over again. A run in his car, and whatever the weather he refused to have the hood up. A halt at an inn, any inn, Molly found. A club—any sort of a club—if they could find one and obtain admission, and what with one thing and another her whole spirit longed for the days and the evenings when the height of her entertainment had been for John to suggest a drive to one or the other of the Homes, and for Miss Spofforth to ask her help in the garden for a while now the lighter evenings were here again.

In the garden spears of crocuses were following the dainty green and white bells of the snowdrops and the now faded Christmas roses. Under the hedgerow Miss Spofforth had planted masses of violets, and as she walked there late one evening, waiting for Ian to arrive, since her instincts told her Miss Spofforth, although always polite, did not really like inviting him into the cottage, the scent of all the growing things, the pulsating, heady triumphant scent of spring, assailed Molly's nostrils.

All at once she began to wonder just what she was doing here.

When Ann had first suggested a holiday 'down on the farm' she had been quite certain she would be disappointed. Town-bred, and a little travelled in her childhood, she had thought she would find life in the sleepy little village boring. To her surprise she had discovered endless delights about which she had never even dreamed, but once the accident had happened her spirits had drooped again until she had been lifted from the confines of Beckside, as it were, into the more spacious—mentally—world of the centre and all its attendant interests.

She looked across at Rosewood Cottage, dreaming in the light of the pale spring sunshine. She felt she owed a great deal to both Miss Spofforth and to Cat, but all at once, like a blow from nowhere, she realised how much of her contentment, so lately and so unexpectedly dispelled, had been due to her contact with John Maitland and the interests he had made his own.

It had never been a habit of Molly's to resent facing the truth about herself, and she faced it squarely now. John Maitland was more than employer as far as she was concerned. Almost without realising it she had identified herself with his interests, both in the group centre and in the life he led outside the surgery and the Doctor's House. His interest in the two homes and in the well-being of his patients and staff alike were now hers, something she had scarcely realised at all until, that very morning, Betty, the sadness at last gone from her eyes and her mouth, had shyly announced that she and Alex Germain were to be married after Lent.

Sharing John's unbounded enthusiasm for this news, Molly had suddenly realised how much they all meant to her, Betty, Olive, Joan, and even Tim Flecker. Of John Maitland she would not think. They were formally polite to each other, in the surgery and out of it, but the old comradeship had gone, and not until this very moment had she known how very much she would miss it, and his friendly smile, which was so seldom there for her benefit now.

She was roused from her contemplation of nature, herself and her newly discovered knowledge of life by the strident sound of Ian's horn as his car drew up at the gate.

"We'll go and beat up Farrowby, shall we?" he said, his eyes dancing mischievously. "I feel like letting everyone here know I've been, and that I've enjoyed myself! It's mainly thanks to you, Molly," he added quietly as he helped her into the seat beside him.

Molly smiled, but said nothing. Once or twice he had attempted to behave in what she thought of as a foolish fashion, but there had been nothing with which she could not cope, and she wasn't frightened. She felt a sudden slight disgust as the way she was using her leisure these days, and felt thankfully that once Ian had gone back to sea she would swallow her pride and ask John what was wrong, offering to return to her work with him at the homes, even if he himself did not suggest her doing so.

They went from place to place in Farrowby, a small but growing township on the edge of the motorway and with a by-pass which helped swell the number of inhabitants every evening and at weekends.

"I know a good place just in the outskirts," Ian said. "It belongs to a pal of mine—at least he was a pal until he won a load of cash in the football pools and decided to live on shore and try to increase what he calls my investment. He'll be pleased to see me, and we can be sure of a good time."

The Saddlebag proved to be an enormous country club which was evidently a flourishing concern, since the wide courtyard was crowded with expensive cars. From within came the sounds of a well organised show band, and Molly, who had loved to dance all her life, felt her toes tapping to the rhythm.

Ignoring the dance hall, Ian went upstairs at once to the rooms labelled 'Gaming'. Molly's heart sank. Once he was interested here he would be likely to spend the evening, but she settled to wait for him, watching the croupier and the players, interested mainly in the play of expression on the various faces.

She saw Ian chatting with a slender young man whose outstanding good looks were spoiled, in her opinion, by a weak mouth and eyes which didn't appear able to focus on any one point above a second. She waited until, after a time, Ian came across and suggested they had a meal.

"I've ordered," he said in a lordly manner. "Hope you like my choice. It's Indian food. I developed a passion for it on my last voyage."

Molly told him she'd never experimented that way, but that she would be willing to try, and on being shown into a small room where a table was set for two, her misgivings, which she had done her best to hide, returned in full force.

She wasn't really aware of what sixth sense warned her against staying, but something did. As the waiter brought in the drinks Ian had apparently already ordered, she excused herself and went to the powder-room at the other end of the stairs.

A glance at her watch confirmed what she hoped was correct in her memory. There were still more than five

minutes before the last bus which passed through Farrowby *and* the three Bronton villages left from the
market-place.

Yet where was the market-place from here? She
wasn't sure, because she had only been to Farrowby three
times, once with John in his car, and now twice with
Ian, and in each case she had been driven into the town
area from off the motorway.

She didn't pause to reason. Ever since she had stood in
the garden of Rosewood Cottage, reflecting, much earlier
that evening, she had been possessed of grave doubts as
to the wisdom of the kind of life she had found herself
leading ever since the first day of the year, the day when
John, for what appeared to be no accountable reason,
had abruptly turned against her.

Molly turned blindly from the wide, brightly lighted
doors of the Saddlebag. She asked a pageboy, a cheeky-
faced youth who stood in the hall, which was the
quickest way to the town.

"It's a bit of a walk, miss," the lad told her, "but if
you follow that path through the trees you'll come out
slap in the middle of Farrowby. Wherever you want to
be, someone'll be able to direct you from there."

Grasping her bag firmly and not even pausing to
wonder whether or not the path was lighted or where it
ultimately led, Molly began to run. The path was fairly
wide at first, and well trodden, but soon the trees seemed
to close overhead, and there were no lights, save the brief
illuminating flashes from cars going by on the road,
apparently somewhere above, on a higher level.

Molly ran as she had not run for years. Her back hurt
badly, and there was the catch of a stitch in her side, but
she felt she would have continued running, and might
even have managed to reach the bus station before the

vehicle moved out, or at least have found a taxi rank, since the hour was not, as yet, too late.

Suddenly she became aware of someone running along the path behind her, and panic—unreasoning, blind panic—took possession of her senses. She didn't even knowingly wonder whether her pursuer was Ian or not. All she wanted to do was to get as far ahead as possible, and into the lights of a town or even a larger village ... anywhere save in the darkness of the trees.

Her right foot caught in an upraised tree root, and before she knew what was happening she had pitched headlong on the still partially frozen earth, bruising herself badly, the breath knocked completely from her body, her back hurting almost as much as it had hurt when she had been thrown from Satan, all those months ago.

CHAPTER SEVEN

SHE felt arms about her, raising her from the prone position into which she had fallen. There was a wiry strength about those arms, but the feel of them was strangely alien, so that instinctively she fought against their hold.

"Steady, Nurse, steady!" Although she didn't recognise the voice she knew she had heard it before, and without realising what she was doing she relaxed, letting the tension and fright flow from her, so that he lifted her lightly and easily, as though she were of no weight at all.

"You don't recognise me, do you?" he said quietly, and as her fright subsided and her heartbeat steadied, she knew him for the tall, slender young man who had been talking to Ian such a short while previously.

"I'm Robert Toft," he said now, "Bob to my friends. I'm Ian's pal, we were shipmates until I won enough for what I wanted to do, and," his voice became softer and the tone a tinge regretful, "I'm not in the least certain I've done the right thing, after all."

Molly didn't say anything. She couldn't have spoken then to have saved her life, but Bob appeared to understand.

"Ian's been telling me about you," he remarked conversationally, taking her arm and walking, half leading her along the path she had just used as an escape route. "I may be wrong," he was saying as they walked, "but it seems to me that whatever joy you were getting from this new job of yours has departed, for some reason or another. If you'd like a change," his tone didn't alter in the least, "just give me a ring. I'm not asking you to do anything you'd hesitate to do, I think," he went on. Now there was a hint of amusement in his voice. "I'm offering you a very good job—an excellent one, in fact—as a receptionist at any one of my three clubs. I've the one where you've been tonight, a little place called the Lighted Candle right in the centre of Farrowby, and another country club, the Scarlet Slipper, out Featherlay way. None of them have any similarity to the other two," he continued. "I'd like you to let me show you the other two before you make up your mind."

Molly remained silent, because she simply didn't know what to say. The path had emerged now into what she recognised vaguely as being the middle of Farrowby market-square, but Bob kept a firm hold of her arm and guided her round the corner.

"I'm looking after you, Nurse," he said lightly. "I only followed because I know Ian's not exactly reliable when he's been drinking a while. When I saw you rushing downstairs I tried to call you, but you were too quick for me. I don't know how badly your back was hurt," he laughed a little, "but there's not much wrong with your legs and your stamina for running! If you hadn't fallen over that tree root I doubt if I'd have been able to catch you, and I'm supposed to be a fit man!"

It seemed wrong to say that fear had lent her both strength and stamina, especially when she hadn't known of what it was she was afraid, but Bob evidently didn't expect an answer, for he went on talking as though he hadn't anticipated a response.

"This house," he commented, pressing an illuminated bellpush placed in an unobtrusive doorway. "I use these people when I do the round of all three places. They're most reliable, and they know me quite well, if you'd like someone to vouch for the fact that I mean you no harm."

"That's all right," Molly said quietly. "I don't . . . I mean . . . I feel you don't intend any harm, and I'm grateful. I was hoping to catch the bus."

"You hadn't a hope," Bob said cheerfully, then, as the door opened and a middle-aged man wearing a dark-blue coat and open-necked white shirt looked out, he stepped forward.

"Mr. Toft!" the man said in evident recognition. "Had you booked us, sir?"

"No, Frank. This is a sort of emergency. This young lady has missed the bus back to Bronton, and I'd like you to take her home for me. You can drop me off on the return trip, if you will."

"Certainly, sir. Where in Bronton, miss?" the man asked. "Bronton itself, or Bronton-by-Water or. . . ."

"Rosewood Cottage," Molly broke in. "Brocks Lane, Bronton, three cottages from the Doctor's House," she added, and wondered why she had done so.

"I know it." Frank disappeared and a moment later came out with his collar on, and wearing the peaked cap of the professional chauffeur. "Usual car, sir?" he queried, and Bob's quiet 'of course', were all the words spoken until, seconds later, Frank brought a gleaming Rover from the garage at the end of the yard, and stood respectfully holding open the door for Molly to enter.

She didn't realise her nervousness had communicated itself to her companion until they had been driven at least three miles and Bob suddenly laughed aloud, proffering a cigarette case.

"Relax, Nurse!" he ordered. "I'm only seeing you safely home, remember! Don't worry about Ian. He'll

play as long as they'll let him, and drink for the same
length of time. One of my boys'll see he's all right, and
he'll be sorry as hell in the morning, but don't let that
worry you! He's sailing the next day, and he'll have to
report tomorrow afternoon at the latest."

"I'm . . . sorry," Molly apologised, and knew he understood she was apologising for her obvious distrust of
himself. Calmly he smoked his cigarette through, tapping
the ash elegantly into the ashtray with one long, well
manicured hand, and all the time he talked.

"I'm not interested in girls," he said firmly. "I've two
sisters I think are marvellous, and they're more than
enough for me in one lifetime. I like girls—don't get me
wrong—but there are so many beautiful ones, so many
kind ones, so many talented ones, I just wouldn't know
what to go for . . . so I appreciate all of your sex and leave
'em strictly alone, except, as I've just suggested to you, if
they can help me improve my business life. I think you'd
make a wonderful receptionist. You've the looks, the
charm, and, I'd stake my life, the kindly human interest
which gets people and makes them want to come back
again and again to the same place, just to talk to you."

Molly didn't know what to say, so, wisely, she said
nothing. This conversation was so unlike anything she
could have imagined, even in her wildest dreams, that she
sat in silence, wondering what was to come next.

"Young Ian hasn't hurt you, has he?" Bob said unexpectedly. "He's a well-meaning lad, but thoughtless. He
doesn't always realise that people take him seriously when
all he wants is a little fun on a shore leave."

"No," Molly smiled in the dim light from the small
lamps above their heads, "Ian hasn't hurt me."

"Then someone else has," Bob said in his forthright
fashion, "and the more fool he."

"It's over now," Molly murmured, but at the same time she felt she was cheating him a little. She was implying she had been hurt by Flint, and that, she knew now, wasn't strictly true. Her *pride* had been hurt, but not the essential Molly. In her innermost heart she *had* been hurt, and it was an astonishing thing to realise that the hurt stemmed from the one man she wouldn't have believed would have hurt a fly ... Doctor John Maitland!

She was so astonished by this discovery that most of what Bob was saying went completely over her head, and the car had glided to a smooth halt before she realised he was awaiting her reply and that she was safely back at Rosewood Cottage once more.

"I said," Bob was a patient man and he smiled into her worried face, "or rather I *was* saying, when you went off into some sort of a daydream and evidently didn't remember I was here, that any of these numbers will reach me. If I'm not wherever you ring they'll let me know and pass on a message. If you'll let me show you my other two places before you make up your mind, I'd be delighted. I'd suggest the Scarlet Slipper first. Just think over all I've said, will you?" he added as he helped her from the car. "The job's yours, and for as long as you'd like it, if you let me know. Oh, and don't worry about your bag, I picked that up and it's here." He held it out and Molly realised she had even forgotten she had dropped it as she fell. "I'll see your coat and anything else comes directly to you," he added. "Good-night."

Molly echoed his good-night and pushed open the gate. Miss Spofforth's light was still burning, and the girl knew she would have to go up and explain to the old lady what had happened before she herself went up to rest. Bob sat beside the driver now, watching her walk along the path and to the door, then with a hand lifted in salute, he spoke to Frank and the big car moved away.

Cat was lying in his basket beside Miss Spofforth's bed. He opened one disapproving eye and stared at Molly, swishing his tail as though in greeting, but he didn't get out of the basket to welcome her home.

"I've left cocoa in the thermos, and a covered plate of snacks," Miss Spofforth began. "I'm glad to see you are evidently all right. Dr. Maitland was more than a little worried when he left."

"Dr. Maitland?" Molly asked, mystified. The old lady nodded, placing a velvet ribbon in her book to mark the page she had reached in her reading.

"And Nurse Jarvis," she named the village midwife with perfect composure. "They've had their work cut out. A woman in one of the caravans up on the common was having a baby, or at least that was the message Nurse Jarvis received. When she got there she found there was more than one child arriving and she sent one of the gypsy boys for Dr. Maitland and here, for you to help. There were four babies altogether. Nurse Jarvis told me all about it, but the details were too much for me to remember. I've never been interested enough in the mysteries of birth to know just what she was saying was so wonderful, except that the old great-grandmother of the clan, tribe, family, whatever they call themselves, was a wonderful help in every way and ought to have been given nursing training in her youth."

"I wish I'd been here," Molly murmured, feeling guilty, but Miss Spofforth looked at her face, noted the lines of strain and formed her own conclusions.

"You don't look as though you've exactly had a good evening out yourself, dear," she said gently. "Get your cocoa and such, and get to bed as quickly as you can. No one in the centre's going to be much use to anyone tomorrow so far as I can see! Doctor's light is still burning. I can see it if I lean back a little, now the leaves aren't fully out on the trees."

She had mentioned this deliberately because she wanted Molly to understand it was highly likely Dr. Maitland was awake and worrying about her. Molly didn't even entertain such an idea for even a second. John's manner towards her since the beginning of the year had been so cool and so formal she was now firmly convinced he regretted his earlier friendliness and interested help. She would have been utterly astonished had she been able to see him at that moment.

When he had run Nurse Jarvis home to the small Nurses' House where she lived in company with her co-midwife-for-the-district, John had set himself to watch and wait, expecting the return of the open sports car in which he had seen Molly drive away so often of late.

The sight of the dark blue and grey limousine which had swished to a halt at the gate of Rosewood Cottage, both startled and dismayed him. He had watched, hating himself for feeling like a spy, as Molly descended from the car and afterwards Bob stood in the roadway, watching until the door of the cottage had closed behind her.

What was she doing? Who was this stranger? Where had she met him, and what had happened to the young man—the cousin of Eric Brent—with whom she had started out for the evening?

These questions and a thousand more chased themselves round and round in his brain. He didn't understand himself in the least since that dreadful hour when, returning from the accident, he had seen Molly standing at the door of Rosewood Cottage, obviously saying good-night to young Flecker.

From that moment, John knew, he had seethed with jealousy, a jealousy for which there was no real reason, and to which he had no real right. Why should this slip of a girl disturb him so greatly and in such a fashion? What business of his was it as to whom she met, where she went or what she did?

"It isn't even logical!" he told himself severely. "She was just a patient, a patient to whom I gave employment because it suited both her purpose and my own, at the time!"

Logic, he found, could be cold comfort. There was no logical reason why he should have found his work at the two Homes of much greater interest when she was beside him; no logical reason why he should have taken a pride as well as an interest in the change in the once despised patient Alex Germain, a pride which gave him a firm sense of achievement when consulted by a very much changed Betty as to the best possible way to transform Alex's shabby home at the other end of Bronton.

"I wouldn't have cared two hoots what happened to the chap if Molly hadn't gone to see if she could help him, and told me what was really wrong," he decided. "She's influenced a lot of people in and around Bronton, and I'm sure most of it has been for the good of all concerned ... but what in the name of heaven has she done to me?"

He went to bed at long last, after Miss Spofforth's light and the light in the adjoining bedroom had gone out, and, apparently, the whole of Bronton slept. The whole of Bronton, save for the doctor!

"This is the end!" he decided, getting up for the second time and descending to make himself a malted milk drink in the hope that he would be soothed sufficiently to drop off. "I shall have to have this out with her in the morning," he resolved. "Either she keeps respectable hours, like the rest of us, or else she takes her town ways somewhere else. This isn't good for her, for me or for the practice!"

Yet although he stormed to himself as he settled to sleep the subconscious part of his mind persisted in revealing the knowledge that it wasn't either his own welfare or Molly's, or even the welfare of the practice which was bothering him. It was simply and solely that, unless he knew where she was, what she was doing and with whom she was spending her leisure time, he could not rest.

He was downstairs and in his consulting room before even Liz had arrived for work. Mrs. Burton worried and wondered, but having seen both John and his father through several emotional crises of varying intensity, did not worry unduly.

"He's in love, bless 'im, and he don't want to acknowledge it," she told the dish-washer, and as the chromium plating winked back at her in silent agreement, she continued talking to the kitchen ware, solving, at least to her own satisfaction, the emotional problems she was certain were besetting her beloved Dr. John.

He buzzed angrily for Molly long before she had time to sort out the appointments for the day, several of them still incoming as Liz coped expertly with the switchboard.

"I trust," he began in the new cold voice he had adopted towards her from the very first day of the new year, "you enjoyed a pleasant evening yesterday?"

"Very, thank you," Molly lied bravely. "I'm sorry I wasn't around when Nurse Jarvis needed help."

"We managed," John said dryly. "No one, you know, is quite indispensable, Molly. Had you not been here at all we should have managed, and manage we did. I must say," he added as she turned to go back to the reception desk, "when you leave the place with one young man and return, not too many hours later escorted by another, one ceases to wonder why your love-life went astray. Perhaps it had something to do with your own misconceptions of loyalty?" and before she could think of an adequate answer he had picked up the telephone on his desk and was dialling briskly.

CHAPTER EIGHT

AFTERWARDS Molly often wondered from where she had gained the strength to carry on that morning. Automatically she answered the imperative sound of his buzzer. Like a sleep-walker she conducted patients to the consulting room and saw them out. Once or twice Joan asked anxiously if anything was wrong, and was rewarded by a faint smile and an assurance that everything was all right, except that Molly had a bit of a headache.

Betty, frankly now a happy person but with a quiet happiness which was as unconforming as her sadness had been, hovered about sympathetically, offering aspirin and saying that Molly should tell Dr. Maitland and get him to prescribe something to ease the pain.

How could she, Molly asked herself wryly, ask him to prescribe something to ease the pain caused by himself and his own words, by his apparently deliberate misunderstanding of the kind of person she really was, the kind she had believed he knew her to be?

When she was due to go off duty she changed into her outdoor things and went off to Rosewood Cottage with nothing more than a brief 'good morning, everyone', and with no specific good morning to anyone, not even to John.

She felt at that moment as though she never wanted to see him again, yet despite the memory of his cutting, hurtful words she knew the most important moment of each and every day was the one when she walked into the reception room and responded to his greeting.

Or it had been her most important moment . . . until this morning. She unlatched the gate of the cottage and walked slowly and dispiritedly along the path. Perhaps because of the unaccustomed exertion of her running the previous evening, her back ached now as badly as it had done when she had first stopped attending the hydrotherapy, and certainly just as much as when the Mobile Unit first came to minister to her at Beckside.

She felt unutterably weary as she opened the door, and Sarah Spofforth, having spent a busy morning in her garden and, as a result, glowing with rosy cheeks and bright eyes after the bracing hours spent in the fresh air, bit back her words of reproof that Molly was, again, just a few minutes late for luncheon.

"Something's wrong," the spinster told herself. "Something's very wrong, and I don't know how to put it right for her, poor child."

Aloud she began to talk of the annuals she had been planting, of the way in which her rose hedge was already bursting forth in a positive riot of buds, with the promise of another summer's beauty ahead, then she pointed to the fragrantly scented flat cakes on the tray on top of the stove.

"I've made some of what my mother used to call oven-bottom cakes," she announced with pride. "One eats them with thick butter and treacle spread over it, and usually warm from the oven. I loved them when I was small, and in spite of all the modern inventions I don't suppose even science has been able to do much about children's taste buds! I've baked those, and I'm keeping them warm, until Nurse Jarvis calls. She says there are swarms of children round those caravans, and I just thought . . ." she paused, her wrinkled face betraying her anxiety to please, "if their mother's ill and there are four new babies to care for, nobody will have much time to bother about the others, not just yet."

"Surely the babies are in the Cottage?" Molly asked, her voice toneless and her words as automatic as though she were publicly announcing that it wasn't of the slightest interest to her.

"No," Miss Spofforth shook her head. "Seems the grandmother and the mother didn't want to be parted from them, and they were so insistent that they could look after everything themselves that Doctor finally gave in, on condition that Nurse Jarvis went up there today and, if she decided it was best, sent for the ambulance to take them—and the mother—into hospital then. I expect," she chuckled, "they'll all be doing surprisingly well. These people seem to have an amazing gift for survival!"

"Common sense says it would be better if they and the mother were in the Cottage," Molly said, not really caring at this point, but talking because this subject seemed safer than most and certainly interested her hostess.

"Common sense is all very well in its place," Miss Spofforth announced unrepentantly. "But there's such a thing as uncommon sense, and I'd prefer to say that was what really counted in the long run. The mother doesn't want to be parted from her children. The grandparents and the father don't trust four walls. Their own instincts are telling them what's the best thing for them and the mother, and I think their own instincts will be the right ones . . . their *un*common sense."

"It doesn't always work out like that," Molly announced, interested in spite of herself. Common sense told her the best thing for her to do right now would be to walk out of Rosewood Cottage and away from Bronton and never come back. But instinct, or what Miss Spofforth called her uncommon sense, told her her only way to real happiness was in walking through this sudden darkness and believing she would find light at the other side.

Before she had time to expound this thought and its implications, there was a tap on the door and a moment later Nurse Jarvis's rosy face was peeping in on them, her upturned nose sniffing appreciatively.

"Takes me back a few years!" she announced, eyeing the cakes. "Granny used to make these for us when we were children. Are they for your tea?" she asked of Sarah with the intimacy of a long-standing friendship.

"Not ours, for the children in the caravans," Miss Spofforth said firmly, packing the still-warm cakes into a thick paper bag and adding a small tin of syrup as a parting gift. "Tell them how to split them and butter them," she advised, adding anxiously, "I expect they have butter?"

"More than you, I fancy," Nurse Jarvis chuckled. "They live very well on the whole, you know. I honestly don't know why people want to clip their wings, cage them up in houses. Let them be free, free as they want to be, and as man was probably intended to be before all the fetters of civilisation got wrapped round him!"

"There have to be fetters, as you call them, Nancy!" Unheard by any of them John had entered the open door and heard the latter part of the conversation. "There has to be a set of rules," he continued, looking steadily at Molly. "If there wasn't a code, life would be a bear-garden, a jungle ... a place where the weakest, or the least able to deceive, would go under. . . ."

Molly could not stand any more. He had spoken as

though his remark was merely a part of the general conversation, a following up of the remarks Nancy Jarvis had made, but her uncommon sense told Molly, in a voice which would not be hushed, that the words and their hurt were intended for her and for her alone.

"Excuse me," she said, turning suddenly and facing him. "I didn't intend to do this in this way, Dr. Maitland," she said formally, "nor did I intend it to be done before my friends. I think it would be as well if you would please accept my notice as from this minute. You said to tell you when I felt I could work elsewhere. I think now is the time to make a change," and before any of them could speak she had turned and rushed headlong upstairs to her own room.

No one spoke or moved. Only Cat, who had been sitting on the hearthrug watching and listening, suddenly returned his leg, which he had been holding in a peculiar position the better to wash it, to its rightful place, and sped after her, as though intent on offering comfort.

"What have you done to her, John?" Sarah Spofforth hadn't used his christian name since his father died and he had officially become 'Doctor Maitland' to the village, but she had known him since he was a child, and now she was once more the older, authoritative friend to whom he had been wont to rush in his schooldays when problems loomed too large for his young mind.

"I . . . I don't really know," he said slowly. "Yes . . . I do," he didn't explain, and Nancy Jarvis, half Miss Spofforth's age and very little John's senior in years, stood uncomfortably, listening to them.

"It's too difficult to go into now." John seemed to be pleading for understanding, and with Sarah he had never previously pleaded in vain. He did not do so now.

"Get along up to the caravan site, both of you," Miss

Spofforth said briskly. "I'll see what's wrong, and if I can help I will. But if you let that girl go from your life and the life of Bronton, you're a normal stupidly blind male," she opined, "and I'd given you credit for having more common sense than that! I thought you'd at least your mother's sense of intuition."

Abashed, John retreated, with Nurse Jarvis carrying the all-important gift of cakes and syrup as well as the bag. He had thought he had that gift too. Never before had he been mistaken in assessing the character of people with whom he had to deal, but this time, he reminded himself grimly, he had seen the evidence of his own misbelief with his own eyes.

"We'll use the one car," he said abruptly, holding open the door for Nancy. "It's not a pleasant drive."

From her window Miss Spofforth watched them go. She was still certain things would work out in the best way for all concerned, but people, she felt, had a dreadful way of trying to manage for themselves and ending in a worse tangle than when they started out! Breathing a silent request for help for her two friends, Sarah started upstairs, and when she tapped on Molly's door, to discover the girl and Cat curled up together on Molly's bed, she did not scold as she would normally have done and pointed out that Cat had his own bed and should keep to it.

"Have they gone?" Molly asked tonelessly, and Sarah could only nod. The girl rose and picked up her handbag, depositing Cat at his mistress's feet from where he leapt lightly to the window seat.

"I'm going to the telephone kiosk on the corner," Molly announced quietly. "I won't phone from here, or from the Doctor's House. That would be cheating. I'm phoning a friend about another job."

164

"What's happened?" Sarah could not keep the anguish or the curiosity from her voice. She *had* to know, if she was going to be able to help them both.

"Doctor John," she said slowly and distinctly so that the hurt in her voice was barely disguised by her tone, "said there's no wonder my love-life went wrong, because I have no conception of loyalty. I don't agree ... but if this is the way in which loyalty is to be rewarded, then I'll place mine elsewhere. I'll be back for dinner, if you don't mind," she smiled a wan smile. "After all, I suppose I shall have to give him a week to find someone else."

Cat sat on the window seat and washed his whiskers. Suddenly overcome by emotion, she picked him up in her arms and hugged him so tightly that he mewed in protest, but they stood together watching Molly's slim figure as she went purposefully down the road to the red-painted kiosk on the corner.

Bob Toft wasn't at the Saddlebag, but a polite young man assured her that she would be able to reach him at the Lighted Candle. Molly consulted the card he had given her and dialled again, and this time she was rewarded by being put through to him almost as soon as she had given her name.

"I've got your coat and things in the car, Nurse," he said. "I can bring them over this afternoon."

"I'll collect them tonight, if you meant what you said about my seeing your three clubs before deciding," Molly said crisply. "I'd like to see the little one you mentioned, where you are now, please. Tonight, after evening surgery."

For some reason she did not tell him she had handed in her notice. Perhaps, she thought subconsciously, she was letting her uncommon sense rule her, but there it was.

He argued for a few minutes, trying to persuade her that the Scarlet Slipper would be the better place for her to see. "It's more your type of background, if you know what I mean," he said, but she was adamant. She didn't know why, but she wanted to see the Lighted Candle and she wanted to see it that very night, before she had time to change her mind.

"I'll have Frank pick you up at Rosewood around eight, then," Bob said before he rang off. "He'll bring you right here, and I'll be waiting to show you the place. We can go on to the Slipper later if you're bored."

Molly felt that if an hour or so in the place was going to be boring then she must be all kinds of a fool to contemplate leaving what was the most absorbing career in the world—even though at present she wasn't really nursing—for something which even its owner admitted might be boring.

"I'll give it a trial, anyhow," she told herself. coming out of the kiosk and setting off for a walk, a walk she had little energy for but one which she felt would at least occupy her, without having to exchange a word with anyone, until it was time to return to the evening appointments.

Evening surgery was busy. There was no time for personalities, but she had a sharp reminder of Tim when a message came from the Poole Dairies, requesting a visit from Dr. Maitland as soon as possible as Mr. Poole had suffered another stroke.

"That's where the girl works that Ann said was once practically engaged to Tim," Molly reflected as she rang the message through. "I wish they could get together again. Evidently they have the same sort of interests."

Joan, she knew, would tell her son, and she could only hope Tim would have sufficient interest in his ex-beloved to go and see if there was anything he could do to help her in this new time of crisis, when so much would obviously depend on the girl keeping a cool head.

She and John exchanged nothing more than bare civilities throughout the hours of surgery. As soon as the last patient had gone, Molly rushed into her outdoor things and fled, startling the rest of them. She was usually the last to leave, even though, since the new year they had all noticed she and John no longer stayed for long periods discussing the cases or visits. Tonight she was off and away with the speed of a hare.

She ate her dinner almost mechanically, and Miss Spofforth, who had devoted much time and energy to its preparation looked in vain for the customary words of appreciation.

"People can't worry about their stomachs and palates when their minds and souls are upset," she told Cat, but even Cat had no comment to make when, minutes later, the big Rover pulled up quietly before the gate. The car had barely stopped when Molly rushed out. Frank opened the door and she was inside the comfortable interior, speeding back towards Farrowby.

This time the car went into a long, narrow street which had been part of the old town. Molly shivered a little as she noted almost automatically the way the tall old houses seemed to lean together as though whispering secrets, and her mind felt strangely revolted when the car swung silently into a covered courtyard at the back of one of these narrow buildings, and Frank opened the door.

Light streamed from a door which suddenly opened and showed the way down some stone steps into what had evidently been a storage cellar to warehouses at some time. Outside she had seen the sign of a lantern, with a candle—she supposed it was plastic and carried an electric bulb as a flame—swinging in the wind.

The Lighted Candle wasn't in the least like the Saddlebag. Here was a different section of the human race. Mostly young people, they sat around in small groups, perched or slumped on a series of either stools or easy chairs, while the dim light from several real candles shone eerily over the scene.

From somewhere muted pop music played, and there was no sign of a show band such as had been giving a non-stop performance at the Saddlebag. Bob appeared to materialise out of the shadows, and soon he was seated opposite to her, at a table very close to what looked like a trapdoor set into the wall.

Nothing about the place appealed to Molly, but she said nothing. Bob flicked his fingers, and expressed his astonishment when she insisted upon drinking nothing more intoxicating than a plain tomato juice.

"Good for the figure, maybe," he laughed, "but not so good for trade! You're setting a bad example."

He talked and laughed and joked as he had done the previous evening, but there was something different in the atmosphere here. The restless gaze she had noticed in his eyes the previous evening seemed to have intensified, and his fingers were restlessly tapping the table in time to the music, almost without ceasing.

Molly's head was aching. She had been miserable all day and tonight she was even more so. She had hoped to escape from her feelings, but now she knew nothing was ever solved by running away. She was about to ask Bob to send her home, when suddenly a tall youth who had been sitting alone at a table in the corner rose to his feet and blew a shrill blast on a whistle. Her mind had merely a second to realise this was a policeman and a police whistle, when she found herself gripped by Bob's arms, much as he had gripped her to lift her up the previous evening, then she was thrust through the trap-door-like opening in the wall and found herself grabbed by another pair of arms, which were instantly identified by Frank's voice as their owner spoke softly but clearly into her ear.

"It's all right, Nurse. Mr. Bob thought they might come tonight, but I'll look after you . . . this way," and before she knew what was his intention she was helped into the small sports car she now recognised as being the one Ian had used while on leave, and they were roaring out of the courtyard by a side passage, and away.

Molly did not speak. If she had been frightened the previous evening when she had first heard Bob running after her, she was now absolutely terrified. Beside her Frank was saying unmentionable things about the few youths who had spoiled everything for everyone else. They, it appeared, were the purveyors of cannabis, the dealers in hemp for smoking, cocaine for sniffing, 'like snuff', as Frank said angrily. There had been talk of hard drugs too, and the local police were determined to join in the national drive to get rid of this evil. "They're so clever," Frank was explaining. "You can't tell who's got 'em. They hide capsules in the daftest places, but they get away with it, and the police *have* to find them in actual possession of the drugs before they can do anything about it. Bet the floor's littered with all sorts of that rubbish, back there, just this minute . . . asking for trouble, that's what it is. Gives a place a bad name," he growled, "an' you can't tell who's dealing in the things . . . that's why the boss didn't want you mixed up in this, and we knew it would come some time. There's been a big drive."

It was at that moment the animal ran across the path. Only weeks later did Molly learn of the quick wrench of the wheel Frank had given as he yielded to his countryman's instinct not to kill the creature. The wheels spun, the car left the road, and, Frank's attention having been diverted already because he had been so intent upon making his passenger see the police raid was nothing to do with Mr. Toft and not by any means the usual sort of thing, he struck the surprisingly solid bulk of a tall, sturdy oak tree growing in the hedgerow along what had once been a Roman Way.

Molly hit her head—or something hit her on the head, she didn't know which—and then there was a whirling blackness which became a whirling redness, then she was sinking down, down, down and into oblivion. The next thing of which she was really fully conscious was of being in a familiar bed and of John standing grimly over her. It was only at this point that she realised she was once more a patient in the Bronton Cottage Hospital, and for the second time in only nine months!

CHAPTER NINE

JOHN seemed relieved when she opened her eyes, and she did not at first recognise that the relief was because, apparently, she was still in full possession of her senses.

"We meet again, where we met the first time," John said in a cool, calm voice. He put out a restraining hand as she tried to sit upright.

"Keep still until I say you may sit up, please," he ordered. "The X-rays show no brain damage, but you're still concussed, and you know enough to realise what *that* means. What on earth," he became suddenly human and angry, "were you doing in that sports car, at that time of the morning, and so far away from Bronton and everyone who knows you . . . or thinks they do!" he ended cryptically.

Molly's head was aching badly, and every bone in her body seemed to be aching intensely, but she could not let that remark go by without protest.

"I'm not even employed by you now, Dr. Maitland, remember?" she said, and her voice seemed to her to be coming from miles away. "And, to the best of my recollection, you were the first to . . . withdraw from our friendship, months ago."

"Because you showed you had other interests!" he could have bitten his tongue out if that would have recalled the words, but it was too late.

"I don't understand you," Molly retorted, and was shocked and amazed by the change in his expression.

"Over Christmas," he said with quiet fury, "you were the perfect companion. Everyone at both Homes thought as I did, then, that you were a wonderful person, and that your heart was large enough to embrace and care for all the worried and misunderstood, the homeless and the helpless people of the world."

"And . . . ?" Molly's curiosity prompted the question as she tried very hard to force her tired mind back to those weeks over three months ago now. "I didn't change!" she emphasised. "You did."

"You went to the Watch Night service with Miss Spofforth," he said accusingly. "Betty was there, and she saw you. She told me afterwards she also saw Tim Flecker come to Rosewood. I wouldn't have believed either her or anyone else, but I saw you myself. You were seeing him off, and it was almost one o'clock on New Year's Day."

"I . . . he . . . I didn't know he was calling," Molly began defensively. Try as she would she could not recall details of that early morning meeting at this point. She only remembered she and Tim had argued, much as she and John were arguing now, and that since then she had scarcely seen Ann's brother, and when she *had* seen him they had found absolutely nothing to say to each other.

"Then you need not have invited him indoors, and with Miss Spofforth safely in bed and quite probably reading!" John said, still angry. "It wasn't just that, though. When you came here you were engaged to one man. He's gone. You've broken free of *that* engagement only to almost run into another, young Flecker would come running if you snapped your fingers, when all the time he'd be a great deal better off with the girl from the dairy farm, Jean what's-her-name. They at least speak the same language! On top of all this you run around with young Brent, although Doctor Brent told you what sort of a man his cousin is. You're not satisfied with all this, you seem intent on breaking the heart of another poor man as well! Seems to be a habit of yours, Molly, and there's no known prescription to cure this sort of thing!"

The prim figure of the woman Molly remembered as being Sister Franklyn came silently to stand beside him. It was as though a mask had dropped over his face, and instantly he was icily self-controlled.

"I think I'll write up a sedative for Nurse Watson, Sister," he said quite calmly and without a trace of the anger which, a few moments previously had appeared to shake him from head to foot. "I shall leave it to you to see she doesn't get excited."

"You're wanted on the phone, Doctor," Sister said as she watched him write the prescription, "It's young Mr. Flecker, and he's phoning from Poole's Dairy Farm."

"He must have gone to be with Jean...." Molly was beginning hopefully, but apparently John wasn't interested. He turned on his heel with a muttered exclamation which might have meant something or have been simply an outward ejaculation which said he washed his hands of her and the whole affair. Molly turned her head into the pillow and let the few tears which seemed to be scalding her eyes slip unheeded down her cheeks.

It all seemed such a waste, all at once. She had come to Bronton, to Beckside Farm, merely with the idea of having a carefree and inexpensive vacation in the home of her best friend. If only she hadn't insisted on riding Satan, then she wouldn't have been hurt, she wouldn't have had to leave Tunby, not even for a short time, and she would never have lost Flint or encountered John Maitland.

She pulled her thoughts together with a jerk which was almost a pain. This was utter nonsense. She and Flint hadn't really anything in common, she recalled. They had more or less drifted together, partnering one another at the regular monthly dances, sharing most of their off-duty times, and gradually everyone, the two of them included, seemed to take it for granted that they were paired. She ought, Molly reflected miserably, to have seen the red light months before she had come to Bronton. She ought to have known when Sir Alistair Grahame's letter first arrived and Flint had leapt so promptly to its call. She ought to have known, when he didn't want her to change her holiday plans so that they could have a vacation together at a later date. And she ought to have known it was all over when he didn't come running to her side as soon as he had known she was hurt.

Thinking back over casual remarks made by one or the other of the patients at the centre, or of those of Miss Spofforth, who although she didn't gossip knew almost all there was to know about everyone in the three villages, she ought to have known too that the disagreement, misunderstanding or whatever it was, between Tim and Jean Purvey was nothing more than a lovers' quarrel, and might well have blown over months ago had she not been an invalid in his mother's house, as well as being his sister's best friend.

"I hope they get together again," she thought, thinking of Tim and of Jean, the girl she didn't know but of whom she had heard such glowing reports. Everyone was filled with admiration for the wonderfully capable and business-like way in which she had taken over the control of the dairy farm when Bill Poole, her employer, suffered his first stroke. From all sides Molly had heard that the dairy farm was doing better now than ever before, and that Bill was so grateful that he had indicated that, if he recovered, Jean should be a full partner in the business.

"And with Beckside and Poole's place running almost

parallel to one another," Molly mused, "that would be ideal."

"I'm to give you this now, Nurse Watson." The girl in her crisp nurse's uniform, standing beside the bed, was someone Molly had not met previously. Like the rest of the people in this area she appeared only too anxious to be friendly.

"I wasn't here when you were a patient of ours the first time," she said, smiling. "That's why you don't know me. I was on holiday too. I've been to Italy, for the first time ... it was gorgeous. ..."

She chatted gently, quietly, as she straightened the pillows and smoothed the bedclothes. Her name, she said, was Norah Speight, and Dr. Maitland had said if she could see to it that Nurse Watson had adequate rest there would be no objection to visitors that evening.

"There's sure to be someone in to see you, Nurse," Norah Speight said in a friendly tone. "There have been no end of enquiries about how you are and how badly hurt you were. You seem to have made more friends around here in the few months you've been with us than most folks do when they've lived around the place for a lifetime."

Molly smiled faintly, hoping the few tear-stains weren't visible. Norah didn't comment, and Molly closed her eyes as though the serative had already started to take effect. She felt rather than saw or heard Norah move away, but behind her closed lids she was picturing all the people she had known and worked with since she had first come to stay in Ann's home.

There was John, of whom she had grown inordinately fond. There were all the people of Beckside, from Sophie down to Billy, who was 'helping and learning', as he had explained on first acquaintance.

Mentally moving from Beckside, she thought of Miss Spofforth, and, of course, Cat. Cat was as much a friend as any person, and he would be wondering why she had not arrived at the cottage at her normal time. Miss Spofforth always swore he could tell the time, she was certain, and although she had laughed at this in the beginning as being a fond woman's fancy, now Molly felt as certain as Cat's mistress that this was so.

From Miss Spofforth her thoughts turned to the Homes, both of them, and their inmates. They, she felt, must have missed her, for she had received loving messages couched in strange terms from the children, and two lovingly worked gifts of a pyjama case and a purse from the Home for the adults.

What did they think was the reason she had ceased to visit them, did they imagine she too had rejected them, adding to their hurt, as so many others had done throughout their lives?

The thought was painful, and she shrank from pursuing it further, but she also shrank from thinking at all of John and instead tried hard to remember how it was she had allowed herself to be drawn into being Ian's companion, thus leading to the present situation where she was 'involved', there was no other word for it, with Bob Toft and his friends.

At this point her tired brain strove to convey the message that if John had possessed the sense to tell her he had seen Tim leaving Rosewood Cottage on the morning of New Year's Day, none of this would have ever happened! But she couldn't think any more about it now, she could only feel her heart must be weeping the tears her eyes denied permission to fall, and at last she fell under the spell of the sedative and slipped into a dreamless and quite exhausting slumber.

Norah Speight woke her some time later, with a first-year nurse accompanying her with Molly's tea on a tray.

"Speciality of the house," Norah joked. "We spoil our special patients! No, the truth is, Miss Spofforth brought these in for you," she lifted the cover from what Molly saw with affection was a plate of the special fairy cakes which the old lady loved to make because Molly enjoyed them so much. "There are some special cress sandwiches as well," Norah went on, "and she'll be popping in to see you later, when your other visitors have left."

"Other visitors?" Molly felt stupid, echoing the other's words in this fashion, but Norah smiled, the understanding type of nurse's smile Molly had used herself a thousand times.

"Lots of people want to see you," she said, "and Sister says if you like I may prop you up a little. You're not to get excited, though, and to eat all your tea! I'll bring your things so that you can pretty yourself up a little when you've eaten."

Obediently—mainly to please the pleasant Norah to whom she had taken an instant liking—Molly ate her tea. Although her head still ached and her back and side hurt more than was comfortable, she felt considerably better as the young nurse brought her handbag and a mirror.

"Nurse Speight says she'll lend you this, Nurse," the girl told her, obviously somewhat awed by the sight of a staff nurse from another hospital lying in one of the Cottage's beds as a patient. "The visitors' bell will be sounding any minute now, and there's more than one to see you!"

Miss Spofforth, her 'church' hat, an elaborate affair made of imitation violets and in the style almost always affected by the late Queen Mary, sailed into the ward.

177

She had a small posy of flowers in her gloved hand, and a little book.

"I couldn't bring very much, love," she said quietly. "We'll make up for all this when we have you back at Rosewood Cottage. I knew you'd like the flowers, and I thought you might find Keats a comfort."

Molly thanked her gravely, wishing she had the secret of the old lady's serenity. As if she understood Miss Spofforth unexpectedly stooped and kissed her.

"Don't be too long in getting well, child," she said quietly. "Cat's wondering what has become of you! Don't worry too much, you've been looking for happiness in all the wrong ways. It's like looking for gold. You have to dig and dig and tunnel for all you're worth to get the gold from the rock, or the diamonds from the mine, but it's worth it in the long run. Looking for happiness is like that. You go on tunnelling and digging your way through masses of rock-like misunderstandings and difficulties, but it's all worth while in the end, when you have the pure gold in your grasp! Keep your faith, love ... don't even think of failure. That's most important. You'll get your reward and just when you don't expect it!"

There was a small commotion going on at the doors of the ward and Miss Spofforth rose stiffly.

"That'll be John, with his party," she said mysteriously. "He said they hadn't given him any peace until he said he'd bring some of them, so I'll leave you now. ... Don't be too long before you're home!"

Molly was still musing over the magical mystery of the word 'home' and what it meant to so many people, when there was a small rush of hushed feet and six of the elder children from the Home came hurrying to her bedside. There was no sign of John Maitland, but each child had a small gift, whether it was a nosegay of violets from the hedgerow, a branch of pussy-willow or a laboriously embroidered handkerchief, each offering, she knew, was made with love.

There was a lump in her throat and she had difficulty in assuring them all she had missed them as greatly as they had evidently missed her visits and that it would not be long before she was visiting them again. She felt overwhelmed, a little humble, and strangely proud and happy all at one and the same time, and it was with this queer mixture of emotions tearing at her that she looked up in time to see Tim and a tall, dark-haired girl with a tanned complexion entering the ward.

"We can't stay many minutes, Molly," Tim said, taking the girl by the hand and leading her to the bedside. "I wanted you to know Jean, and to be the first—apart from Mum, of course—to know we're going to be married the same week as Betty Taylor and Mr. Germain. Won't you wish us luck?"

"The very best of luck and from the bottom of my heart," Molly said sincerely. "It's the best news I've heard for some time. I know you'll both be happy."

"And so will you, one day, Molly!" Tim said with such conviction that she was almost inclined to believe him, although as yet she could not see any reason at all for doing so.

"I'm . . . happy now," she said, and was surprised to find she was. Except for the fact that John had shown not the slightest interest in her welfare beyond that of the normal doctor with any patient, he had not shown she meant anything to him at all, she still felt not exactly happiness but a strange new kind of contentment which was very close to happiness itself.

The bell rang again and the visitors began to stream

out of the ward. Nurses bustled about as the time drew near for the day staff to hand over their charges for the night staff to care for, and Norah Speight left the drinks trolley to a younger nurse and came to stand beside Molly's bed.

"Dr. John asked me to find out if there is anything you'll be wanting especially," she said quietly. "He's most emphatic that we should look after you well. And," she smiled faintly, "a most gorgeous sheaf of hothouse roses arrived a little while ago. I've put them in the flower room until morning. I didn't think you would particularly want to see them tonight. The card on them simply says 'Bob'. I thought you'd like to know."

"Thank you." Molly's eyes stung with tears again. She willed them away, desperately reminding herself that a weepy patient was often a nuisance, but she felt so weak, so stupid, and she couldn't even think of ever having a faith even remotely approaching that of the elderly spinster whose home she had shared for so long.

"Don't cry," Norah said quietly and surprisingly. "*You* have no need to cry. It's Dr. Maitland I'm sorry for."

"Dr. Maitland?" Molly's eyes dried themselves as though by magic and instead of feeling sorry for herself she was suddenly consumed by curiosity as to why anyone should feel sorry for the doctor. He had, or appeared to have, everything to make life both happy and comfortable. Why did he need sympathy? "Why?" she asked point-blank.

"Well," Norah took one look at Sister and evidently decided it was all right to talk. Dr. John, Molly thought wryly, was a favourite with all the nursing staff at the Cottage, and if Sister thought Nurse Speight was helping the doctor, then she would look the other way!

"He was jilted, you know," Norah said quietly and as casually as though she had said he had the 'flu. "I'd just started my training, and he'd just taken over from his father, although Dr. Maitland senior was still alive, but practically helpless. He contracted paralysis agitans, you know, and Dr. John and Mrs. Burton, and Annie Phipps—she had just retired as District Supervisor—looked after him. Dr. John was engaged to a girl whose father owned the huge bulb farms and nurseries just outside Farrowby. They were happy enough, or so it seemed, until she went on an export tour of the States and so forth. When she came back she was *married* ... and he didn't know anything at all about it until she rang him up and told him why she hadn't let him know which plane to meet."

"How awful!" Molly's generous heart rushed out in waves of sympathy. No wonder he had appeared to understand when Flint.... She would not pursue that thought, not even for a moment.

"What happened?" she asked.

"Nothing very spectacular," Norah said. "He simply went on with his work, but he was quieter, and he never joined in any of the social activities that go on round here. There are quite a few things, you know, hunt balls, Mayoral banquets and so forth and all sorts of things like that, but he never attended any other function afterwards. People said he was afraid of meeting Elaine ... that was her name, but I don't think it was that at all. He'd just decided no one was to be trusted, and when his father died he lived alone in the Doctor's House, except for Mrs. Burton and Sam Baker who does the garden and things. He helped found the two homes, but that seemed more for something to do than for any other reason. He never had anything to do with anyone, except as a patient, until you came to Beckside, although he was always a friend to everyone in all three villages."

"And I think he trusted me," Molly said quietly, and was amazed by the fervour of the other girl's response.

"He did," she said firmly. "Everyone was so pleased when you two began going around together, when he took to driving you to the two homes, and things like that. He was laughing more too, and instead of simply looking after people's health he began to take an interest in their welfare as people as well as patients. We all thought. . . ."

She stopped, her cheeks reddening, and rose to leave.

"Now you know," she said awkwardly, "why I'm sorry for Dr. Maitland. It doesn't seem fair the same thing should have had to happen to someone like him twice."

"But I didn't . . . I mean I haven't . . . we weren't like that at all," Molly began, but Norah was young and she had the hurtful tactless truth of the young.

"You've given your notice, haven't you?" she said clearly. "I know, because Nurse Jarvis told my mum. And that's why I'm sorry for the doctor more than I am for you, but I'm still sorry for you, Nurse . . . you just don't know what you've thrown away!"

CHAPTER TEN

IT was neither her aching head nor the pain in her back which kept Molly awake that night. She had thought the phrase 'heartbreak' was a catch phrase used by the few romantic writers she had read. Now she knew there was more than a scrap of truth in those words.

She turned and tossed more than a little, and stout, motherly Nurse Betts at last rose from her place by the desk in the middle of the ward and moved quietly over to Molly's bedside.

"Is the pain very bad, Nurse?" she whispered. "Would you like me to get Dr. Knowles to write something up for you?"

"No, thank you," Molly whispered back, adding before she could prevent the words popping out: "Don't you ever make a cuppa in the ward kitchen at night?"

"Coming up," Margaret Betts nodded in a conspiratorial fashion. "I could just fancy one myself. The others won't wake, and I'll chat a bit if you like. We're not too busy tonight. Do you ever have your night duties so peaceful?"

"Not often," Molly confessed. "But Tunby's a much bigger hospital."

A junior nurse brought the tea some minutes later, and Margaret, glad of the opportunity to chat for a minute or two with this girl about whom all the villages were talking, sat companionably with her as they sipped the hot, comforting liquid.

"Don't take too much notice of what people say or

think, Nurse," Margaret advised abruptly, and, it seemed, without any particular meaning. "In small places like Bronton there isn't much else to occupy one's mind except what's going on around one, whether it's of general interest or not. I'd not be in too big a hurry to go away if I were you. I'm a great believer in sticking things out . . . my neck in particular," she said, half laughing as she gathered up their cups. "I shan't be offended if you tell me to mind my own business, but try to remember what I've said!"

Molly lay back and tried to will her thoughts to stop whirling and to compose herself to sleep. She remembered what her mother had once told her about a disturbed time she had gone through.

"I used to imagine I was sinking into a sort of deep, deep bed of soft feathers, or a still, quiet pool," she had said. "There was a star at the top. I used to fix my eyes on this imaginary star and feel myself sinking, sinking until the feathers—or the water—closed over me and I felt supported, strangely and strongly supported, by some unseen power. It's a habit once acquired one can't lose. It taught me the truth of the words from the Bible . . . 'underneath are the everlasting arms', and I've never doubted since that day."

Remembering her mother and the various difficult times she had endured throughout her lifetime, Molly made herself think of those words over and over again. It was true, she recognised dimly, as her thoughts grew sleep bemused. There *was* a strength, a strength which was not of the body, perhaps not even of the mind, but of something else, which she could *feel* reaching up to her—or was it down to her?—and supporting her, whether she would or not.

She sighed and, without knowing it, relaxed. Gradually

her eyes closed and remained closed, and when next Margaret made her round she saw the nurse from out of the village was soundly and sweetly asleep.

She was awakened by the day staff coming on duty, and, knowing it was all part of the routine, made no objection to the early morning wash and far too early cup of tea.

"Post's in," the cheerful young nurse who helped her wash stated laughingly. "Mrs. Flecker left this for you as she went by. I think she's been up to the dairy farm. She certainly wasn't on her way to the centre as early as this!"

Molly took the envelope and stared at it. There was no mistake. The handwriting on the envelope was Ann's, and the letter had obviously been enclosed with her weekly one to her mother which Joan would have received yesterday.

Feeling curiously as though Ann's world at Tunby General and her own here in Bronton were more than poles apart, Molly slit the flap of the envelope and drew out the single sheet of hospital notepaper with the writing in Ann's neat style and careless phraseology which was so typical of her friend.

"Thought you'd like to know," she had written after expressing the hope that Molly was getting stronger, "that your ex-friend Flint has decamped and is on the first rung of the ladder to Harley Street and the private clinic he covets so much. He left last week."

There was a great deal more, but the remainder, so far as Molly's awareness went, amounted to nothing more than social chit-chat and didn't really count for anything. That one sentence was all that interested her just now, and as she lay back and remembered how, almost publicly, she had given John notice that she was leaving, her cheeks burned and she wanted to hide before he came round the Cottage as was his wont three mornings of each week.

Try as she would she could not remember whether or not this was one of those mornings, and she would not ask anyone! She knew now what she must do. There wasn't any other way. If he wished she were not going, he would have to come to Tunby and say so. It would be too humiliating to go back and to ask if she might retract her notice when she had announced it before Miss Spofforth *and* Nurse Jarvis ... and when so many other people evidently knew all about it.

She thought and thought, but no alternative entered her mind. He hadn't asked her to stay, and when she had opened her eyes in the Cottage his greeting had scarcely been what one could call either friendly or sympathetic, much less lover-like.

"He'll be glad to see the back of me!" she decided. "I'll write now ... and get someone to post it before I change my mind."

She had a ballpoint pen in her handbag, and a junior nurse brought her some paper. Feeling the best she could do lying propped up in bed would not really make a good impression, she spent a long time carefully composing a letter to the Matron at Tunby, asking if there was anything she could do in her old hospital, administrative or otherwise which would come under the heading of light duties for a further six months or so. By that time, her experience told her, she should be well enough to go back on to the wards.

It took a long time to write the letter to her satisfaction, and when the junior came round with the mid-morning drinks tray, she asked if Nurse Speight would be on duty that day.

"She's doing a split shift," the junior said. "She's on now, but she's been in with Sister nearly all morning. Would you like me to tell her you'd like to see her before she goes off duty after lunch?"

"Please." Molly felt strangely like a junior herself as she spoke. Gone was the feeling of strength she had felt in the night. Now she felt alone and strangely frightened, frightened of what Matron might say, frightened there wouldn't be a place for her after all, and frightened most of all because she knew at the bottom of her heart she didn't in the least want to go back to the hurly burly of the town life and the busy hospital ever again. What she wanted now was to work in this village community, amongst the people she had grown to know and to love. The trouble with somewhere like Tunby General, she decided, was that apart from the chronics no one ever stayed long enough in the place to get to know them, and the staff was so huge—being in proportion to the size of the hospital and to the population of the area—she didn't know everyone as she felt she did here. Even Ian's cousin, Dr. Brent, was better known to her than some of the staff amongst whom she had worked for years.

Deliberately she pushed these thoughts to the back of her mind, and when Norah Speight came to stand beside her bed she was quiet and composed, the letter in her handbag, neatly sealed in the envelope the junior had obtained from some source of her own.

"What can I do for you, Nurse?" Norah asked, and although Molly didn't recognise it at the time, being too blinded by the misery of her own decision, there was compassion in the dark brown eyes of the other girl as she looked down at her.

"What time are you off duty?" Molly asked, knowing quite well.

"Two," Norah said briefly. "Why?"

"Would you please post this for me, then?" Molly held out the envelope and some coppers. "I've written 'first class mail' in the left-hand corner, and here's the money ... sorry I had no stamps in my purse. I generally carry some."

"I'll get one," Norah said steadily, examining the envelope before slipping it away down the front of her apron and securing it in some way known only to the profession.

"You're going, then?" she asked the question casually, but she was watching Molly carefully as she spoke.

"I can't do any other now, can I?" Molly said quietly. "I've more or less burned my boats."

"I'll attend to it," Norah said, and only afterwards did Molly remember that she had not said "I'll post it for you."

She lay back when Norah had gone, wondering who, if anyone, would come in to see her that evening. The excitement had died down. The roses Bob had sent stood in their full glory on the table in the centre of the ward, and in small bowls, grouped round that magnificent display, were the little posies brought by the children from the Home and by Miss Spofforth.

Norah, moving one of the small bowls as she passed, remembered the old lady's face when she had walked up the ward to sit beside her boarder. Miss Spofforth had taught Norah at Sunday School, and like almost everyone of her age in the three villages the girl had a great respect for the old lady's wisdom. She did not say anything to anyone, but when she left the Cottage, instead of turning left and going home, she turned right and walked the long road back to the cottage which stood near the Doctor's House.

Sarah was in the garden. Cat, sunning himself by the door, rose to his feet and came to investigate the newcomer. When he discovered she was not Molly he turned away and chased an early butterfly, losing interest in someone he did not know and possibly feeling disappointed the girl he had come to look upon as another member of the household had not returned after all.

Sarah, ever polite, invited Norah into the Cottage and made some tea.

"It's something about Molly . . . Nurse Watson, isn't it?" she prompted after the formalities had been concluded and Norah sat there, not quite certain how to begin. Without a word Norah took the envelope from her handbag and held it out for Miss Spofforth to read the address.

"I think she's asked if she can go back there," Norah said, adding in a little rush of words: "I don't think she wants to go, Miss Spofforth. She told me all about what had happened when we were talking the other night. If Doctor Maitland had known *why* she was seeing Tim Flecker off on New Year's morning, and if he'd known *why* she went out with Dr. Brent's cousin . . . and if he'd understood how shut out she's felt ever since. . . ."

" 'If ifs and buts were apples and nuts. . . .' " Miss Spofforth muttered softly, "there'd be a great deal of difference in the way people ran their lives! I've forgotten the rest of that rhyme, but it's sense. Ifs and buts get no one anywhere. It's action . . . and to have action one must have faith the action is right. . . . Wait here a minute, will you? I shan't be long. There's more tea in the pot and a fresh cake on the table. Help yourself . . . back in a minute!"

Without even bothering to put on a hat—a most unusual thing where Miss Spofforth was concerned—she picked up the letter and went out, closing the door behind her. Cat, who had followed them both indoors sat and watched the newcomer. Norah felt discomfited. She didn't much care for his unwinking stare.

In less than five minutes the old lady was back, a somewhat flustered-looking Dr. Maitland following at her heels.

"It's there," she pointed triumphantly at the envelope which lay where she had left it, on the table. "Ask Norah what she thinks. She doesn't believe Molly wants to go—and neither do I. She wants to stay, to settle here where she's been so happy . . . and so miserable. It's time you both took a good look at yourselves and remembered it's always as well to find out *why* someone does such and such a thing than to accuse them of having done whatever it is for the wrong reason! Why don't you ask her, John? Ask her what she was doing at the door that morning and why she went off with young Brent. Ask her what she was doing running away from that Saddlebag place, and how she came to be in a car when the police were raiding that little den of foolishness in Farrowby! You know none of it is in the least like the Molly either of us know. There must be some reason for all this somewhere. A girl like that—one who loves, yes, loves—the folks in the Homes as much as you do yourself doesn't suddenly step right out of character like that without a reason, and she doesn't go on and on about the delights of living where the air's clean and pure, and where everyone's so friendly and then rush back to the town life she told me she dreaded living again! Ask her . . . before we post the letter. That's the least you can do!"

John sat down heavily and stared at the innocent-looking envelope. He knew he had been hurt—and because he was hurt he had wanted to hurt in retaliation—and he had, he knew, said some cutting things! Now he was shocked from his anger. He could see in imagination Molly as he had first seen her, after her accident with the horse. Molly, who had been shattered by Flint's cruelty, just as he had been hurt by Elaine, but Molly hadn't allowed it to sour her life.

She'd worked at the centre as hard as any of them. She'd helped in both his beloved Homes. She'd done any and everything he'd asked of her, and yet—he was white with self-scorn—he hadn't felt able to trust her.

He rose and picked up the envelope, half bowing in a quaintly old-fashioned way to the astonished Norah.

"Can you keep Miss Spofforth and Cat company for a short time, Nurse, please?" he asked. "I promise I won't keep you waiting long." At the door he turned and smiled at the old lady. "I haven't done this since you made me apologise to Cook when I was a child," he said with a sad smile. "That seems a lifetime ago, but you assured me she'd accept my apology and we'd be better friends for it! You were right . . . what do you say this time?"

"Exactly the same," Miss Spofforth said equably, "if you say what is in your heart and don't talk with your tongue in your cheek. It will be all right," she said firmly, and, confident in her own Unseen Help, she was sure it would be.

Molly had given up trying to read the magazine Nurse Betts had left for her, and was lying with her eyes closed, trying to recapture the feeling of sinking into oblivion which she had managed the night before. Only that way, for a time, she felt, would she find not peace exactly, but a quietitude of mind...and that would have to be enough until she had time to get over all this.

She opened her eyes as he looked down on her, sensing his presence at her bedside. Her heart began to hammer painfully, and she struggled to sit up, but he drew a chair nearer and took possession of her hands as they lay outside the bedclothes and on the coverlet.

"Molly," he said, and there was the tenderness of all the world in the one word, "can you ever forgive me? I don't even want to know why, if you don't want to tell me. I should have known you better. I should have known you well enough to have trusted you...and I didn't."

"Do you *now*?" was all Molly said, and as he nodded it was as though a lighted lamp illuminated her features and her smile was the one he had hoped for but never expected to see there, just for himself alone. That smile held all the love, all the trust and all the loyalty he could ever hope for in this world or the next, and regardless of the interested gaze of patients alike, he leaned down and gathered her to his heart.

"Can you bear to stay here, in Bronton, darling," he asked against her hair, "not just the group centre's secretary but as the doctor's wife...for a lifetime's job?"

"I couldn't bear not to," Molly said softly, truthfully, and he knew now that Miss Spofforth had been right, and that everything had worked out rightly for both of them after all.